Close Your Eyes and Think of Dublin:

Portrait of a Girl

Illinois State University / Fiction Collective Two

On the Edge: New Womens Fiction

Also Available in the Series

#1 Cris Mazza, *Is It Sexual Harassment Yet?*

Close Your Eyes and Think of Dublin:

Portrait of a Girl

Kathryn Thompson

FICTION
COLLECTIVE
TWO

Normal • Boulder

Published by Fiction Collective Two and Illinois State
University, with additional support given by the Publications Center of the University of Colorado at Boulder,
the Illinois Arts Council, and the National Endowment
for the Arts.

Address all inquiries to: Fiction Collective Two, c/o
English Department, Illinois State University, Normal,
Illinois 61761

Acknowledgements:

Novel excerpts have appeared in these publications-

• *Blue Light Red Light*, New York, NY, Spring 1991.
• *Center Magazine*, Center Press, Santa Fe, NM, 1991.
• *Black Ice*, University of Colorado Publications Center,
   Boulder, CO, Spring 1990.
• *Fiction International*, San Diego State University
   Press, San Diego, CA, Spring 1990.
• *Portland Review*, Portland, OR, Spring 1990.
• *The Cream City Review*, University of Wisconsin,
   Milwaukee, WI, Winter 1988.
• *Wisconsin Review*, University of Wisconsin, Oshkosh,
   WI, Winter 1988.
• *The Quarterly: The Magazine of American Writing*,
   Vintage Books, A division of Random House, New
   York, NY, 1991.

Thompson, Kathryn
  Close Your Eyes and Think of Dublin: Portrait of a Girl
On the Edge: New Womens Fiction #2

ISBN: 0-932511-41-4
ISBN: 0-932511-42-2

Manufactured in the United States of America.

Distributed by the Talman Company.

For my mother and father

CONTENTS

"The words which are criticized
as dirty are old Saxon words known
to almost all men and, I venture, to
many women..."

Judge Woolsey

Madeline soon ate and drank.
On her bed there was a crank,
and a crack on the ceiling had the habit
of sometimes looking like a rabbit.
(VISITORS FROM TWO TO FOUR)
"read a sign outside her door."

Every Good Boy Does Fine

"In an old house in Paris
that was covered with vines
lived twelve little girls in two straight lines.
In two straight lines they broke their bread
and brushed their teeth
and went to bed.
They smiled at the good
and frowned at the bad
and sometimes they were very sad."

I was born a small baby extrapolating in the dark. Like Gregor and baby tuckoo I awoke to find an insect in my bed, *of which I could form no clear conception.* I was given a princess phone and drove a little pink car for mary kay cosmetics. A mobile of prehensile shapes and sizes frightened me into premature speech.

My wide yowling vowels, A E I O and U, could not be distinguished from the music and the whole crib was brimming with cape light. I knew the jingling eyesore over my head was no constellation; who but the infant tuckoo knew the pilot's last words retrieved from the bawling black box of the downed jet; heard dogs and black widows spinning gossamer booties for cats; fathoms deep, who but fishes and amphibious polyglots in cribs knew the virtuoso in the kitchen to be her mother. Two drums bass beat in the tympanum of my frantic ambition, and I could *follow the bouncing ball.*

Portrait of a Girl

Long long ago, peering under the dangling pant leg of an amputee named Dane, I knew I shouldn't but I was not ashamed.

Brawling and pink I wrote *mack the knife* over and over, pulling from the taffy the still pulsing ganglia. (These days, a good friend must be activated with remote control from across the country.)

Why after all these years devoted to its indigence, it turns to you with a job and some money and says *you're not my mother—I'm cosmetically changed.*

Years later it walks away beautifully, insulted by its own intelligence; because you cared for it, it is antipathetic to you, serves you last.

Visibly moved by its delusory corporate spirit, dazed by a peculiar sense of poetic justice, you blurt out your secrets to your engaged friends and lead with an excerpt from an actual poem.

Skipping along a speckled roadway with my tiny satchel and blow torch.

I'd remembered what I'd seen.

Like Elvis he had a pulse in the corner of his lip and it kept time with the music. When I arrived at his house at 9:00 a.m. he was sweating and ill-prepared. I thought he was Superman and he changed into Clark Kent for our lessons. He pushed his glasses up on his nose and he would raise his eyebrows, one, then the other; when he walked he was bull-frogged; his legs pulled apart like the bow of a violin. He cracked the case open and the ray of pink cape light came back into the room. He slid the bow of the violin up and down the cake of rosin. The bow hair he told me, was imported from Siberia and nothing could have been more delicate. The top is spruce the back is maple the black ebony wood is from Africa this here is pernambuco wood from South America. Never touch the bow hair with your fingers he told me, and I could feel him watching me each time I unsnapped my case and prepared the bow.

That first lesson (grabbing it with my fingers) he had erupted telling me never to do that again and I hadn't liked him and I'd felt hurt and humiliated because I hadn't known. But those were the precious words Italians had for the very particular way they wanted a thing done. He paid strict attention to the way I treated my instrument and postured that with one hour a day the music would evolve. (I imagined it was the fine hair of a small animal still alive and I never again touched it with my fingers because its mother would never again pick it up.)

First he dipped his bow into the vintage rosin, then he tucked his Stradivarius under his chin and waited for a long time before he began to play. He cocked his wrist, his eyes flowed with the milk of a perverse kindness, and then he began; a whole rest, and then he began again: *pianissimo, mezzo piano, piano; Arco,* he said, use the bow; *forte, mezzo forte, fortissimo; pizzicato,* he said, pluck with the pointer finger of the right hand: *ritard* and *diminuendo.* He said *allegro* and that meant fast.

A tiny ball of spittle appeared on his lip when he finished that word. I liked that. All the virtuosos in my life had a kind of pleasing halitosis.

When he popped a string he replaced it deftly and *legato* smoothly and with another in his case. He delicately loosened the bow hair after playing and gently set it in its case. His guttural wife said *Mr. Mastrianna* like he was a man who did wonderful and secret things and she was always thanking him, not fawning, but thanking him, and it was something I knew even then, the way he played her

11

like his violin, indifferent to her, but dedicated to her happiness.

He always patted the case when he put it away and I imagined on certain occasions when I was not there he kissed it on the rump.

Indifferent to my suffering, no signs of love or recognition, he simply said *play that G flat*. He issued commands like a short order cook but I always got that look of deadpan ecstasy when I got it right. My last lesson he became my first malignancy, my first man.

He ran his bow over the bridge of the violin to the juxtaposition of skin and bone and when his fingers got to the soft gully at the bottom of the throat, it no longer felt like a throat. A part of me would fibrillate and jerk and die, rising up against itself, again and again, as he commandeered the notes across the strings; washing up like a jellyfish before his feet, I found myself crawling up his trouser leg, making illicit and beautiful sounds; he was keeping twotime and the whole room was brimming with the sound of his shoe.

Your turn, he said.

His little pinky a clef.

His wife in the kitchen.

I was decomposing, approaching, laden or light—converging or diverging—I might ejaculate or ooze—palpitate or pool— I could not—feel my arm.

C'mon, he said, and he resumed playing *maestoso*, in his stately, majestic manner.

I got all flustered and had to pee and I had no courage to ask.

I began to play haltingly. Three quarter time signature, he said, three counts in a measure and how many counts for a quarter note?

In a moment of panic I could not remember the items on the tray. It was a question made to ridicule me; he, too, was telling me to stop slouching, to stand up straight.

Move the elbow up, he said, lifting it gently with two forefingers. He made me count time aloud 1 2 an 3 4 an 1 2 an 3 an 4 an 1 2 an 3 an 4 1 an 2 an 3 an 4 1 an 2 an 3 an 4 an it was no use. When his foot went up, mine came down. When he said 3 I said 4. Soon he was stomping and gesticulating wildly: *one* and *two* and *three four* and... *Can you see that* he said and I reached for my eyes but the sockets were empty.

(A man in a white high collar tethered to his throat had thrown back the grille, waiting for my silence to be heard and my mind scrambled as I struggled to recreate the letter names of the spaces and lines; I could not remember how many beats to an eighth note how many quarter notes in a half note how many whole notes in an eighth note and it all confused me, seemed a lot of complex algebra my bow grazing two strings at a time, perturbed voices gobbling in from everywhere; I couldn't even breathe in time and I was sure if I held my breath my heart would slur my speech.)

I could not see the colors as I knew they had been, crisp and clear, irrefutably, there at the reef. I wondered if I might be the forlorn receptacle of some rare palsy or disease; the muscles I used to dignify or disguise my mistakes were suddenly spastic or unreliable.

I felt again for my eyes but touched my feet.

It had finally happened, I had caught myself inside out in the hood of my sweatshirt, locked myself into the confessional door, and the ones who would find me would not let me out.

Portrait of a Girl

I waited for the silence to deplete itself, a churlish monkey jumping up and down, and he told me to go home. Worst of all, it seemed, he did not understand the singular nature of the rare and noble affliction that rendered me objectionable for now but indispensable to the future, not only to his Sunday morning orchestra but to all mankind. It seemed he mistook these gray episodes for some obligatory state through which all pupils passed at some preordained stage in their perfunctory lessons, and through which all musicians passed, tongue-in-cheek, into virtuosos. (As if I had no philosophical recourse but to play out each page, botch it up, master it, go on to the next.)

I was assigned to go back over my written exercises.

In his divine unction he decreed that I had not prospered or perfected myself or even advanced that week, but that I had somehow *regressed.*

It was true that even as the notes appeared immutable and irrevocable before me, they would not yield to their comprehensive meaning yet remain themselves—separately, distinctly, acutely but concurrently and the more I tried the more unaccomplished the effect; as if I had never played them, never suffered them as I knew I had, and I was not a girl but a caricature of a girl struggling to move the elbow, up, up.

The punishment got worse, too, just as the bow of the violin seemed most encumbered; all my mistakes unforgivable and the very sound of the maestro himself more strained and less sweet. Guided by his consummate presiding intelligence and all-consuming knowledge, prodded by stratagems for playing, guidelines, rules of thumb, places for the elbows and eyes, I played one last and unrequited tune, a sound not loved or understood, which, like the driven snow, I knew would never meet its pristine self in the first person singular, anyhow.

14

I believe I played nothing as plausibly as I played the G string that first lesson with the two of them watching me. He had taken out his handkerchief to wipe the smudge off my violin. Crisp and clear, the irrefutable leafs, the sounds of the strings, had been there, one after the next, each one discovered for the first time.

It irked me most when he prescribed for me what he prescribed for the others.

I banged the violin into the case, squeezing the prized hairs with my belligerent fingers, not bothering to lay the rosin into its velvet sachet; wondering what it was of a personal nature that had so willfully offended him, prompting him to resort to such unfair and retaliatory politics.

I first felt ashamed and than I despised the man who had done this to me, who lacked the elite understanding of my sacred condition, who now reminded me again, as if I had not heard the first time, that I was to review my lesson again, and who knew that, in a puling polite voice, I would thank him for his trouble.

I thanked him and went to perish in the arms of his wife.

Even before I had left the music room my brother had unpacked and assembled his trumpet and begun to play, without fear or retribution. So sure he was of himself that he seemed beyond judgement or reproach, scoffing at reprisals, indifferent to his failed achievements and each week getting better. He swaggered where some ulterior compensating force always let me down (he had once argued to me that god was a *man*), and serenaded by the hoghorn of his trumpet, like a chirping midget with bowed legs, I ambled out of the music room, wanting to spit on myself.

As I clicked shut the door it was still there in the imp of his face; he did not know that the organist must first become a keypunch operator because no one ever told him he would first have to be a *wife*. That he would have to swing in slow circles, his hips rocking back and forth like huge billows, slow, reluctant, out of rhythm, one slow bowl of jiggling marmalade.

It was horrible. It was servile. It was obscene. (All eyes riveted on his sordid struggle to become human. To have to play the *violin*.)

I told myself over and over again and again that it was he who was disavowed in not knowing enough to blush in front of the maestro or his violin. That it was I who played for god's Divine: the philharmonic, the chipmunks at Christmas; for daddy to come home. Whistling Lassie home. Alone.

Yet it was I who first had to be told to begin and then reassured, in order to go on. And when I played it right my breath snagged and I felt stricken rather than relieved, as if the whole gaggle of girls who lived facetiously inside of me had conjoined to say something, and when I failed it was not only my own hapless failure but that of my godless aspirations, my indigent teacher, my disappointed mother and father; and again my misery spoke to the whole exalted world, to some unconscionable audience who I both despised and stood desperate to appease, and finally I terrorized myself with the recognition that it was not my own misery that mattered but only the cognizance of others, the disappointed narcissism of the maestro that mattered and the charms of his expectant wife.

Although I begged for a set of drums, I got some masochistic satisfaction in knowing that my parents would never permit me to look like that. And as my heart pounded away, the one simpering thought that compelled me was that I had ruined everything, leaving a fermenting ball of saliva on the enclosure of his lip.

Meandering into the kitchen, already hoarding her tender venison licks, it disgusted me further that in my impacted independence what I desired most was empathy and kisses; and in my impudence, somebody to talk to; in my ferocity, a benign word; but all I could mutter under my breath were a few smut words: *stupid violin, Mastrianna breath.*

For her I climbed into my snowsuit, let her lean down to pick me up, fluff me up, eat me, *abominable marshmallow*—free of the responsibility of speech—my mouth muckled shut by the one mung bean. Could you sponsor this child lady this large pair of wet dachshund eyes one marshmallow puff (girl or boy dollar a day)?

It was not like being passed like a sweet gherkin to the grandmothers. She was the wife of the violin teacher. She was a harpist and she excited me, too.

I coveted those exquisite moments those thirty odd moments every week when I came to her from my lesson (her husband), swollen, sleepworn, voluptuous, still oozing the warm brown jism of earth, yes, delirious in my pajamas, the burning minty feeling of toothpaste still on my chin. Like a cat stretching, the slight catch before the yawn, the curl of the tongue, the slow thaw before the crack of the ice, the soft flaring of the hare's nostrils, moments with her were—well, I skipped pancakes on Saturdays to eat with her.

I thought she was the safari woman who taught Koko the gorilla his first human words.

Each morning as I emerged to see the table set, her waiting for me or she sweeping over the table like one of the arias from Madame Butterfly or something *especial* like that, I looked forward to it very much.

Like in school, our mass trip to the lavatory, when we lined up, two abreast, into the stalls, giggling, pulling up our underpants, stepping on the bottom rail of the sprinkler sink, pushing up the soap dispenser, sliming and sluicing our pink chubby hands together, it was a pleasant feeling. Each morning as she sat there waiting for me, it was as if she had reached into my ear and licked it.

Swilling her bloody mary and laying the celery fondly on my plate, she would say sit down, honey, and have some eggs with me please. *Honey*, she would say, with me, *please*. She always had a small saucer of tabasco and she dipped each egg into it before sliding it into her mouth. It pleased me that she did not pour the tabasco on the eggs. When she had rolled her tongue a full 360 degrees around the egg, she swallowed it. When she was done she always tapped ostensibly at the corners of her mouth and I jumped up to clear the table.

Men never did these things; men ate for themselves, they did not eat you lavishly, with the eggs. I had never seen the violin teacher eat but I knew he was the one exception. He had an Italian mother who stirred her spaghetti *legato*, smoothly, and he watched her add the last basil leaf simmering *witha* big wide *Umberto* eyes.

I still sat there, enjoying the velveteen, almost runny consistency of her eggs, and she was scraping dishes at the sink.

She was European, she had lichens and moss under her underarms, smelled of mushrooms and figs, and perhaps some exotic fruit I had never tasted. She was big boned, with long, sinewy arms and a palpable bicep. Her breath was always spicy, but not bad. She got very close to your face when she spoke, her chest was always moist and flushed and when she spoke she heaved. I was always very cognizant of her being there, next to me, leaning over me, the rasping quality of her voice, her gentleness with children.

Sometimes she got very close, her breast brushing against me, and I would push back against it and she would get very stiff and very quiet and then she would pull away. I think she wanted to moan. She seemed very helpless at the time. (She didn't have any children of her own.)

When I was ten I lived like that, inside the pitching breasts of wild horses (I got that way around adults).

She thought it was wonderful that I was a child, wonderful that I was a swimmer, wonderful that I was a girl. She spoke to the cats. She was kind to the maid.

I sometimes imagined us together, at the elfin age of eight, brownies and bluebirds planted around the campfire, comfy, still, like marshmallows on the toasty edges of adolescence, a sash of smiles—the two of us—singing Kumbaya! Kumbaya! Kumbaya! My Lord!

Mr. Mastrianna never alluded to my special relationship with his wife. But he knew.

It was a world built not by hands but by words.

There was an art to being an adorable little merkin; one simply said the right things, one simply learned the dogma of one's particular teacher to grow up and become a venerable adult. I had no such aspirations. There was a certain character full of unction and self-importance without insight or self-knowledge whose footsteps you heard in the corridor, years later, telling you to desist. They were the ones who put that sneering diabolical distance between you and god, who habitually separated the girls and boys; the Jesuit who taught only one thing, the woman who took only yes or no for an answer. And I suppose I became importunate as a child as a precaution against those who had no vocation to tell me anything they themselves did not wish me to know.

(Because I hated a face with an immutable calm I once reached across the table to take from a fancy hat the one plume. His wife, she had always been gregarious, I never trusted her.)

I refrained from asking the pertinent question because I saw my nemesis, starboard, flagging me down from across the room.

For the time being I was content to be the sultry intelligence nobody understood. There was always somebody willing to like you as you were. She didn't treat my torrid disease like the inclement weather, and I liked that.

I dressed up like a lady for Halloween, some forlorn lamé joke, just like you, I told her and she laughed.

She liked it when I talked about school. How stupid the teachers, how many times we were told (of such inanities as raising one's hand and marching straight to the little boy's room or the little girl's room in the event that one had to pee very badly in the event that one was a girl). Twice a day we were marched off to the lavatory like a flat chain of paper dolls superficially attached at the hands and feet; the kids who couldn't hold it this long would have problems in later life, my mother had told me, and I told the maestro's wife.

Teachers were stupid they thought we should wet our pants over butterfly collections and gerbils and scream, or something, when it was our row's turn for library on wheels and when they asked stupid riddles you said *I give up* and when they said *knock-knock* you said *who's there* and if you didn't laugh they thought you were *dumb* (didn't get the joke) but I just laid my head on the desk until I was told to sit up because I was plum *bored*.

I smelled the playdough, fresh dittos, anything you could snarf up your nostrils or smear on your face but the gerbil cage outright *stunk*.

Sometimes you could raise your desktop and pretend you were looking for something else. You could examine what was left from last year in a quick, rudimentary way: coins (pennies, mostly), fairies, paper clips, dustbunnies, broken pencil points, an apple core, shavings, seeds and pits, pencil erasures (the kind that make the black smidgens), and maybe something weird like a sugar cube, if some diabetic kid had sat there.

I told her of my classmates who sat prepared and erect in the first row, crayon boxes and pencil points all aligned, bawling or sitting timid and moroselike, not filching or searching, not rising to meander, but sitting, waiting for instructions, living unexamined and exemplary lives.

Still, it pleased me when, to get to the sugar, I had to rise up on my tippytoes to see.

I complained that I could never find but five girls to field a baseball team over recess and they were pitiful; I knew this or I would have made the boys relinquish their claim to the hardball field; being that we had only five girls, two of whom were downright spastic and petrified of boys, anyway, I didn't have a cause.

It infuriated me that girls could be so impish and polite on a ballfield and there were always some girls who spent recess in the lavatory, giddy and stupid, making the whole business of their wasted and insipid lunchhour what the boys were doing. Others looked around for things to plunk on teacher's desk or tugged at the skirts of the lunchladies, or went to the science room to coo at the gerbils or at Visad; Visad was homesick, he was from India. Some of the girls who were very fat or very ugly stood around the doors, waiting for the bell to ring, while other girls danced around them, calling them names, fat or ugly.

I wouldn't run stupid just because some boy came at me I wouldn't say Glick! or Blee! because of some stupid bug just so some stupid boy would like me.

I was the pitcher and when I came off the mound to the bench I was strong and proud and heroic. I believed I could take the Pennant in '78 and when I gave my 3 cents to the milklady, I took my own milk from the carton, shook it, drank it, crushed it, and hit the wastepaperbasket from the third row.

My heroes were the geniuses who were not appreciated in their lifetimes, "the girl who could not talk simply to people, so fierce was her desire to influence them for good."

I told her about kiddycamp, where on rainy days we played crab soccer and kept that giant obnoxious ball aloft, smelling of hundreds of little feet, and watched the RED BALLOON, kiddieporn; the stupid little boy who chased the damn fool thing all over Paris.

I did not tell her about my secret games of Thumper and *Duck Duck Goose*; doctoring a small boy's forget-me-not in grade two. (Afterwards, going into the woods for the best pee of my prepubescent life.)

But at this, our last meeting, I realized—she knew.

And the horse at the riding school had thrown me because he knew, too.

Things happened to me imperceptibly and over time; yes, I awoke one morning to find them there. For so long I had eaten coyly the bonbons handed to me, blushed at compliments, deftly risen up on my tippytoes to see over the counter, zealously completed the find-the-fish puzzles on the placemat, eaten child's portions; had consigned myself to living out my childhood making the necessary concessions, until the time came, as mother had put it, to speak when not spoken to, subvert my curiosity and nonsense for the good of all concerned; I had played the prima donna in the baby bunting, suffered the obligatory flattery, platitudes, salutatory remarks, and reprimands with stoicism and machismo, pretending to remind myself not to take more than I could eat, every year putting my teeth together for the school photograph; then, suddenly, inexplicably, I became hot and angry and incapacitated by the lady who tweaked my cheeks, who spoke to my mother and not to me, and everything they had ever said was twisted, tongue-in-cheek, some kind of weird irony, or lies.

My awkwardness before her became unbearable, and with the sounds coming out of the violin, my cognizance grew. When she touched me, I felt humiliated. Perhaps she knew what I had written, in a panic of meaning and love— frantic pathetic needy love poems—perhaps they spoke of me, together, had heard the ravings of my heart, a rhapsody coming from my enlarged violin.

There was a new urgency to our meetings, but I found I could not walk across the room because they were on the periphery, egging me on. It was a moment of greed, I wanted to cry out but my mouth was muckled shut by the one mung bean; I was hungry, maw-mouthed, I could not eat; I wanted to tell her, there is someone in my bed, the funny little men who live inside, grandmother with whiskers; but somehow language detracted from my ability to speak; I refused to eat; I slapped things into my mouth: cold pickled fish, embryo of squid, slabs of meat, polliwogs, wet clams, slimy oyster bellies, fingers, toes, dollops, a glob of vanilla extract. I dreamed of oysters, hairy, on the half-shell, and a fat king who fucked his food.

Portrait of a Girl

When I got to the table I did not know where to sit. My life had become a horrible game of musical chairs.

I dreamed that he would go to her at night and like Beowulf she would speak that awful Gaelic. I felt a kind of censure, a welling up, a deepening, spreading, sensation, as she sat there, eating her eggs, meticulous, as usual.

My brother had told me he had seen another lady in the house who straddled a viola and planted her two feet like she was a man.

I was no longer the extrovert I was, I could no longer look her in the eyes. For many years I had the peripheral vision of a sheepdog (there was nothing human about me; my hair was most often in my dinner or in my eyes).

I wanted to tell her I had lost my ear for the infrasonic; heard the spindle fibers rearranging themselves equatorially (in huge alterworlds) not hair by hair but sliver by sliver, gathered in switches, cackling, drawn back like a schoolgirl's pigtails or witches' broom; perhaps it was louder, yet; perhaps they were gathered in bales. She would think I was crazy but the cats heard: it is only metaphase and I was a student of the biological sciences.

I found that my tongue betrayed me when I most wanted to speak. It seemed the more carefully aligned my words the more befuddled I became; it seemed I suffered years in the inept pause before the stutterer gains control of the next word. I was no longer able to play by ear. I was not yet able to read lips. My life had an awkward length.

I carried an extra chromosome and soon all the mongoloids were smiling at me with frightening clarity.

Her eyes seemed riveted and stuck on me.

I learned History and the whole past was the same— hunter-gatherer—cowboy-indian—where somebody got the arrow and somebody got the gun. You knew. When teacher handed out the percussion instruments, who would get one.

When the chore was to be done outside, who would go. Who would ride sidesaddle and who got the whole horse. Mathematicians told us coy stories about a hypothetical couple living in base ten. Man was the positive charge. Woman was the negative charge (his overeager opposite, his mate). Mankind, of course, the absolute value (neutral, he maintained), but why the man was always himself, the woman having to spontaneously convert back and forth, in and out of brackets, nobody bothered to ask.

I wanted to be boysleuth, boywonder; there were parts for Dalmatians I never had. He was never as analogous to you as you were to him. (Here, I will squat to pick the berries, and you can run around the house yelling Alyoop!)

We took Hygiene and he took Health.

Lifting the hood of the trash I saw it, Planck's constant, my grandparents, the Mr. and Mrs. T, the fussy eaters (the shuffling benefactors of this dream). What are you doing (out here in the trash) my mother asked and they jumped out, stood like two sentinels, two frankfurters, by a giant can of pork 'n' beans.

In school we studied Art and Literature and I saw two black men standing by the trash eating marbles and playing hangman with a stick horse. They emptied the trash into the belly of the beast and I could hear this mashing and howling and a lot of little legs kicking up, *the nature of which I could not understand.* An old picasso rode in on his stick horse, pulled an eye out of a milk carton, telling me it was only a dream—only graffiti, nihilism, cubism, pop art. It frightened me, the metallic taste of the aroused womb, the clairvoyance of children, the jingling constellation. But he would be back when I was old enough to understand, with the results of my ink blot test.

I dreamed of flautists and animals half goat half man, chimeras, a pontiff, hermaphrodites, Pan and man. I both

25

perpetuated and repelled the violence against me. Monkeys played the accordion, men in skirts played bagpipes, toothless cornpone played harmonica, ladies straddled viola, aborigines pounded tom-tom, rockers plugged into the electric guitar, brownies and bluebirds sang around the campfire, prigs sat at the upstairs organ. But I knew, even then, only the evil in me was free and alone at night I was man in his obdurate blackest.

—was it the dreaded bifida—my spine inching away—

I wished I could wake up and forget everything. Picked up by the nape of the neck and carried off. (The Yankee pitcher would give me an old ball with his name on it. Mother would be there to tell him thank you, mister, and hope you take the pennant this year.)

In the wake of my intrepid fantasies and grandiose inquisitions I had but one entry in my pubescent diary: Mother won at Scrabble again: zemstvo. My pimples are getting worse. I hope Stephen likes me. The boys get to do everything. I bet zemstvo isn't even a word.

I was sensitive, a child with scoliosis, afraid of the deformities I carried and where it would take me. A narcissist, goon, picker of toenails. I taught myself lessons in the dark. I became gross and insipid-looking, a cyclops in heat, one of the flailing Gorgon sisters. I could not—culminate the moment—I did not know—how.

I lived in fear that my own nipples would erupt out of my chemise and she would look at them and then at me.

Her breath was caustic, rancheros, and I was weak. When she spoke to me I felt dense and effusive, molten and stupid. They were prized and dreaded moments and like a tightening sphincter I was too afraid to move. Recovering from the recurrent anticlimax of having said the wrong thing or nothing at all, I would lope off and die alone, content to have my silence mistook for serenity.

She had to pry open my lips to kiss me; my lips were two prongs.

Maybe she thought she was god because she had a face blank and beautiful like the tabla rosa. Well, I don't care *how* she eats her eggs, I told myself, you can keep your moody husband and your stupid look.

I became sad, remote—testy.

Some days I came and went without looking up.

My body became more of an encumbrance over time.

My fingers smelled like they shouldn't. (And perhaps he knew, he smelled it on the frog of the bow, knew I had violated the scrolls and nuts of that winged instrument.) It had made me clumsy, pigeon-toed or knock-kneed, one or the other, unable to keep time, irritable and impatient, blind or worse; no longer the family aficionado; he saw how I'd ruined everything with my bad attitude, my dirty dreams, my furtive eyes, my sick jealousy and longing.

I no longer could play the violin and where I kneeled to pray I felt some persistent itchiness, a slow, unpleasant thaw. Answers no longer came to me pointed and perfected like the isosceles triangle, at church and before bed; and I wasn't sure anymore, what it was I was trying to do; was it a question, plea, or apology; was it penitence, repentance, contrition, compunction, or remorse; was I supposed to read the music left to right or up and down or listen to it and then hear it or wait for it or stomp it out with my foot and scare the children. I didn't know and it seemed that even in my retiring miserable form I had offended everyone.

Mother came in the car still running saying hurryup, pronto on the double the parking lot is jampacked the car's outfront middle of the road and I've got to get dad his supper. We had to stop on the way home so I could use the ladies room and she was very angry and wanted very badly to know: why I hadn't gone before I left. Crying, crying, and in a confused tailspin, I disdainfully told my mother *he would not let me go.*

No creature on earth was more evil, lying to its mother.

Mother posited that it was my dirty business and that I was to call Mr. Mastrianna myself, first thing in the morning, tell him why I had quit, because I was lazy and impudent and wouldn't practice, that my father worked very hard (an OBGYN man) and couldn't come home nights to listen to that damn thing; those are ambitious accusations for a young lady who doesn't practice her violin, my father had told me.

I called at 9:00 a.m. when both he and his wife were giving lessons and gave the message to the Chinese cleaning lady who I had heard on occasion patter in mousy mousy and click the front door shut on the hour, poking her head into the living room to say she was solly. At first I rattled on, indifferent to her suffering and goaded by the blind urgency of the job I had to do. Suddenly overcome with the squalor of her voice as she struggled to take the message— so terrified was she that she would botch the message—I became stupefied by her senses and my English got a little worse. swo down pwease. swo down pwease.

Like an unwanted pigeon all that slid off my lips was dribble and coo. But she was no better.

We were the benefactors of some neutral and impersonal third party, to whom we were held accountable, for whom we were consigned to take or leave the message, and neither of us had any inkling of what we ourselves wanted to say, only what we wanted conveyed to our privileged interlocutor.

(She embarked on her rendition, gushing and insensible, of enny minny miny mo, catch a dolla by the toe if he holla let him go out goes Y-O-U?)

A kind of piety, devoid of belief.

It could not be called pornographic (no one there to watch it).

For a moment it seemed that I, too, no longer had a native language.

I knew that we would never be clean as the tale: the old man and the sea, the boy and his dog, a man and his fish; always the girl and her diamond, the girl and her man. We are the catch, cast off like pink chum to feed the others whose weathered bodies, fore and aft, steady like a ballast, navigate the sea; scratching from their beards a scrimshaw so pure it speaks for itself, white as knuckles, worn as shells, with talons free as a gull's. And we are the virgins on the bow whose blue boobs honking guide the fleet through the night. And we are the dirty little mermaids, flapping our tails to the sailors and shimmying off. And we are waiting under the dock, imperceptible but for the one blip or bubble that rises from our sealed lips when he shows up.

The tusk of an elephant, the weather vane on a New England house, the face on a die, a man in a hammock, the footprint of a dinosaur, a rock on the moon, each man himself, a Tarzan in the primal role; his face carved into the mountain, etched into the caves at Lascaux with the wooly bison, he stands orthodox and alone: in overalls, chaps, breeches or mutton chops; cassocks, loincloths, monkeysuits; stands immutable and irrevocable before you, like a bowl of fruit, a wheelbarrow; incantation, insect, eye.

When he sees his compatriot he slaps him on the back, a starting quarterback, a mason laying one brick on the next. Words plunk down like four by fours. Sticking out a big hulking hand with that suave executive swept back blue silver fox hair; he is a gladiator in his shining epaulets. When he hits the corner pocket the brothers slap him five, and breasts were built for the male remark. (Swooning, you will try to wriggle free from your parentheses; stolen by Paris, you inadvertently start the Trojan War with your beauty.)

The lost and bleating sound of her voice reminded me that the most heinous crimes are committed in god's name.

Before she hung up she said okey dokey.

I knew that behind her sickening devotion she loathed herself and hadn't a notion why. I hung up, my eyes swollen shut; I cried again for her and for me and for all women whose odious job it was to take the message. Hoping, perhaps, that I would someday inhabit the spaces where the female was implied.

When Mr. Mastrianna called back that afternoon, as I knew he would, I stood behind the bathroom door, sucking in my breath, paralyzed as my mother told him frankly of my refusal to practice, of the sanctity of the doctor's home, of the finality of her decision. I thought of myself standing cool and insensate before the cashier to whom mother spoke, waiting for change and not inclined to say a thing; I knew I was no match for mother, the way she jostled by the other shoppers to get to the sale items, kept conversation flowing briskly at the register. My voice was not changing, exactly, but had turned harsh and shrill and sometimes I believe I cackled. I could never tell the lady what it was I wanted. In my benign helplessness I could only babble of going to Nicaragua to help the poor.

I punished myself with an impish politeness, a cuteness, if you will.

I went out to a drive-in that night. Against the sprawling surrealist billboard I fought them off, the Houyhnhnms, human in form and brutish in behavior; chivalry, warmon-

gering, panty raids, harmless pranks of tits and ass, that
boy sniggering of sex; went home, wearily slid my hand into
my jeans, dreaming of rosin and catgut the scrotumsmelling
biscuits, the maestro Mastrianna; the hard creases in my
fingers still there from the strings. Same old plot: millions
of motile sperm and the one stationary, suffering egg.
    The voice said to me then: now baby tuckoo like Mr.
Gregor, *Every Good Boy Does Fine*. That's it, I thought to
myself, FACE and Every Good Boy Does Fine. The names
of the strings were GDAE.

    Unlike Gregor and baby tuckoo I awoke at thirteen
again to find an insect in my bed, had to get to know its
numerous legs, *the nature of which I could not understand.*

Corndog

"Tiptoeing with solemn face,
with some flowers and a vase,
in they walked and then said, 'Ahhh,'
when they saw the toys and candy
and the dollhouse from Papa."

When he saw me standing in the schoolyard that first afternoon, his penis rose like half a worm. Because I was part of his ephemeral gastronomy, he mopped his face, rubbed the glitch in his gelatinous belly and said Harumph. He had Santa's whiskers, an oily corpulence, a flat ass.

I knew instinctively that I had saved myself for this man. But to win his contempt, I had to first outdo the femininity of other women.

His hands were lumpy, gouty, tumorous, and the outdoor cafes were full of him: the ballpark solidarity of the aging lech. When he was not with them he was with me.

He was too kind. He assured me he was not a tits and assman like his friends. He liked me for what little I was.

In fact, he admitted he was partial to little girls. (He is the man you fear when you walk into the elevator. He follows you into the forest and stalks you alone. He moves in packs. It is his hairy prehensile knuckles that grab you from behind. He is the georgia parasol and the uncle who fucks you.) It was his avuncular aspect, his boyish pranks, his impish jocularity, his armadillo boots, that made me love him as I did.

That first night out he opened the door, took my coat, sat me, smelled my wine, picked up the tab. He brought with him the anecdote, the flower, the man. He was a funny man, a true comedian; quick to point out the fly doing the breaststroke in the waiter's soup; honked his nose to finish up a good laugh; kept pulling hankies from his nose. He insisted on the finest accoutrements; gave me bras and burmese neck rings, and heart-shaped underpants.

I couldn't stop staring at his mouth; it was a kind of blind pouch—a coelum—an inverted innard of sorts—a primitive gut, an old oozing war wound, perhaps. (Yes, he had been injured in the war; he suffered from acromegaly, tremors, and tic doloreux, tourette syndrome and hyperthyroidism; he had goiters, abscesses, pustules, and more!) He had the features of a tube worm but he did not lack mouth anus or gut. His words seemed stunted; slowly, grunting and pushing, he moved words upward with a kind of peristalsis, giving his speech a thick, bovine, residual quality. He breathed through mouth, nose, and stoma. His words were not miscible in sentences (but language is so rarely an opaque medium!)

He had seen the world; he was a man whose face was at each moment being ostensibly gutted by a corrosive pizza. Pausing to sop his bread, he told me about the war, the turkish baths, girlie magazines, myasthenia gravis. He had a darkroom and a wide angle lens. He drank cheap whiskey and promised to help me with my career; I could become a hand and foot model for Sears & Roebuck. You have such smooth skin he would tell me and it seemed to me that no man had ever said such a beautiful thing to a girl before. With a wide smile and prominent molars and the enthusiasm of a fuller brush salesman, he popped open a briefcase full of mail order blow-up dolls and oriental wives. He looked so important sitting there, with all his totes and collapsibles.

He made brilliant conjectures about the gene pool: jews japs wops bitches kikes dykes dwarves faggots commies

fraternal twins wives and children you name it he knew
them all and he could prove with machismo and mathematics the superiority of the race, species, sex. He threw open
his coat, and there you have it! All true! Larger than life!
(like a carpenter with his tools) And he pumped his
antebellum tattoo of mother giving head to a forlorn soldier.
You didn't want to anthropomorphize the man but he was
quite a ladies man; he went to Nam; his apartment was
strewn with socks, he saw his enemies everywhere; he
could not face the PTA vigilantes or vengeful mothers but
he could face me! Still, he was a brave man and vowed he
would bomb the abortion clinics, for his wife or children.

He had a dumpy, supersaturated face and these things
made him more distinguished, yet. His throat was tethered, he had a gobbling adam's apple; he had a low brow and
from across the table he watched me, as through a periscope.
He looked so intently at me his eyes bulged with tiny
tributaries of red vein; he paid me constant attentions and
I fell in love with the uncontrollable jackhammer motions
of his legs, his obscene vocalizations, the mucosal churnings,
the incessant throat-clearing; always a jerk blink twitch
grind grope up or down in and out side to side the man was
incorrigible! He could not sit still!

When the waitress went by he jumped up like a man
from a manhole cover, and with the persistence of the whole
Department of Public Works, accosted her with his rubber
lips. He filched poked pinched the waitress ummm harumph
argh ahhah! he said, just a look or a touch, a cop or a feel;
please, he said, I am man; he kept pounding pummelling
the salt and pepper; he was a well rounded man, a man of
the romance languages and the biological urges. Oh! and
if you were a man, you would know! (other women wanted
him too—making him all the more dear to me!)

When I pleased him altogether, he promised to stay away from the sultry black bitches with the lucite sandals. But it is not easy for a man. He had seen the blowjobs on betamax and knew he was entitled, too.

Is that jack-up jive grinding his pecker into the jukebox bothering you he asked. He was kind to ask. He would not let the others at me. Would not have my body wrested from him with wolf whistles, stares and subterfuge, innuendo or catcalls, hardhats on coffeebreak dribbling bologna, the backwash of black men with mouths full of marbles.

When he wanted to make love he got my attention from across the room, squared me between the eyes with a peashooter, shook his testicles, or just lumbered over, plunked down on me, and inserted himself. Sometimes he made a bristling noise in my ear (a moment to treasure!); told me to keep my shoes on or to wear this or that, or to take off my clothes so he could try them on. Imagine! The excitement! In a moment of tenderness he might commandeer a rubber duck across the tub. In my most exquisite moment I was commanded to suck or to swallow and I knew then I would never enjoy pleasing myself as much as I enjoyed pleasing him.

Afterwards he always squeezed my hand, catapulted out of bed; a man, romantic by nature, who believed in chivalry, that men should be men; and in a moment of reverie and longing I ceased to exist for myself but for him, saying to myself the ring! the ring! if only! (I could give him a woman's touch. A cache of smells in every room! Rosettes in the bathroom! Potted plants! This pacified me, like when he looked up at the waiter and said she'll have the *corndog* or when he got that job and said, *we'll move to Ohio!*)

But I did not want to eat. I preferred watching him eat!

I loved to watch him when he slept; such a hulking biped in his boxer shorts! He was the male animal, the whole horse, flubbering his lips, wetting the cottony or webby substance on the pad of his tongue, like an old man flapping his gums. Lying next to me, the man in the alka seltzer commercial—there, in my bed!

Whether he was a pipsqueak or a juggernaut I did not care, he was a man and it was true: his penis was my nemesis, and I felt it, sitting there on the bed, all goosebumps and welts. Pitter patter went my heart! Vaboom went my tonsils into the back of my throat! Oh! how he always left me on the wet spot, breathing irregularly!

Oh! and when he awoke! I was there, handing him the toothpick, so he could pick from his public feces, the perfect corns (yes my mountain flower and first I put my arms around him yes and drew him down to me so he could feel my breasts all perfume yes and because his heart was going like mad and yes I said yes I will Yes)

Yes you are Humbert Humbert and I was your yes yes girl.

Analogous and Miniature Organs

"They left the house
at half past nine
in two straight lines
in rain
or shine—
the smallest one was Madeline."

If I could only hold that arabesque on the cake, keep one heel in the air, a rose clenched between my teeth, making castrating and superfluous remarks, and still emerge from that beauty box singing—a lady diva, a prima ballerina—an object of perfection and silence and censure, and if I should stay in the boiling pot of the natives, a Yorkshire village, a flailing miniature in Kong's hand, cowering in curd's way, sawed in half, the magician's helper, the magician's boobs; I would remain, the gameshow hostess who points to the prize, a Gothic bride.

Minced words fly out of the flytrap. She closes up when there is no man left in the room to admire her. Signs herself Currer, Ellis, or Acton Bell; Bodacious Tatas, or XXX. (She is a perfect hourglass and a wife, and some say she still haunts the upstairs with her unfinished Business.)

And if I should rise like Caesar to give that murderer a name, and extricate the brat Branwell from the home, what man would marry me then?

The dominatrix of language lives alone with her dog Keeper. Her eyesight ruined. The ghost of the Brontës lies with her on the daybed, a he-she; dreaming of the pseudonym, not the name.

(italics, mine)

Portrait of a Girl

I could presume to sit like the lady poets sat devout
among the birdbaths and magdalene lawn statues, tapping
little ostrich wisps of feet together in the mealy-mouthed
moors. To wait demurely for the right word to fly in like a
bird for a fleeting second before it lands on the pinprick of
the finger and lifts off. The lost face inlaid in the locket, the
face retrieved from the attic, years later, the book clutched
to a heaving bosom, the vignette crumbling, dried flower
and castor oil, from its sepia place; the miniature, the
morsel, the facsimile: Charlotte and Emily and Ann, the
anticlimax on the cameo's face, who dragged for centuries
the woodplank leg through the engorged moors.

The moors are filled with tubular suckers, the blueprints of bugs, ferrets, salamanders, weasels, chimney
sweeps; peppermints, scotchies and oriental wives; averted
eyes, places to hide; pickpockets, forget-me-nots, half a
worm; fuss and convalescence, cutthroat aunts, proprietors,
pilferers, schnapps; floral patterns; hunches, pawns,
marbles, fine china; the haves and have nots; sweet 'n' low,
a chef salad; clitoridectomies and cinched waists; corsets,
marmosets, minnie the mouse and thumbelina and a little
world of porndom; ladies molting skins, wigs, lashes; cu-
ticles and hair; the mole on Calcutta's face; truss and
bustle; carapace and countenance and corset; physiogno-
mies, not faces; bodices and bric-a-brac; there is pastina
and muffled cusp of artichoke; the beans are French cut;
there are pug dogs, gentlemen callers, infirmities, thoughts;
the suicidal poets; galoshes, midwifery, dotage and doodle,
the sisters abigail and ann; one chamberpot; little snatches
of movement and color; narcissists, dollops and goons,
pickers of toenails. Earwigs. Usurpers. A rib.

Shall I return home, stick the red newt under the butter
plate, meet in daddy's graveyard after supper, where cura-
tor, beekeeper and librarian once a week meet in their

chaise loungers, inventing the Dewey Decimal System? Like mushrooms sporing, carrying on their own private reproductive lives; shall I feast on tiny benedictine eggs, smear the fire eyes of fruitflies on my melba toast? Like Emma (enema, I call her, Austen's miniature, Austen's mute) my mind a bust, covered and brooding like the furniture, a piece of decorum, I could sign the bridal register, catch the bouquet, pass the revolving tray of confections, pink or lime rosettes, petits-fours, finger foods, tarts and sweets (help yourselves, ladies and pug dogs, to the mots juste, each one its own doily, its own logic; the tray is full of killing kindnesses, madame, choose them all). My own words are antipathetic to me, serve me last. I who never owned a watch or an umbrella, upturn the tray.

At one point in my life it did not seem improbable or implausible or even offensive to study crustaceans or the breasts and beaks of birds, but the gender of things seems to me what the atom is all about. Like Hester Prynne and St. Joan I find I am the real woman all dressed up in men's words; you've got to get to know the scrolls and nuts of the instrument that defiles you, eats you alive; got to know woman the animal, woman the organism, woman the man.

(I said that.)

Outside the moors, the men are running the bulls of Pamplona.

And you can find me whistling, alone, at night, in bars. (no virgin ever wrote no book) I have decided not to jump out of the cake, a pair of lips; a pair of carnivorous licking lips, not even its own lips, not even its own passion or its own anger.

I am sorry that father is dying of consumption and that brother has contracted those dreadful Initials abroad. I have to go. And if I should speak madly or out of turn, beg me to go on, do.

I force myself to watch as one more boy comes of age on the TV, in the classroom, on the football field. (Remember ladies, that I speak to that crapulous and offensive monkey on your shoulder, and not to you.)

How do I enter the realms of the clinically genderless, disrupt the underworld of consensual male meaning, overturn the blackjack tables, bust through the saloon doors, a freelance sheriff in a coon hat; sit at the roundtable, become one of the minds of the generation—old geezer at the bar, panning for teeth; spew the wet phlegmy expletives, the louies and ralphs of toothless men chewing tobacco on their own benches; suck stone, sign that declaration yea or nea, ptooey and blat just like that, call to raise the ante, buy the bar a drink; storm out of the dugouts and trenches, strong and proud and heroic, the child I was, no longer circled by conestoga wagons full of fratboys drinking brewskies and talking beaver; the piano maid in the corner, suffocating in her own boobs.

The mule's balls swung pendulously. A tumbleweed blew across the lonely road.

I am Otto Plath's daughter.

I carry purse like pigskin.

I have my way with words.

Your stumpy fingers could only scratch our heads and tell us WHO GETS THE GIRL. This is not about your middle-aged wife, her yawns magnanimous and disgusting; the one nation indivisible, three divine sons, christ, buddha, allah, awe; beef jerky, the billiard room, scotch on the rocks, warming up in the bullpen; boxing, bullfighting, j.o., t & a, little bug-eye boys who yell BOOBS; Jim Beam, the gestapo, god, breaking wind; politics, boywonder and his wisecracking penis; barefoot and pregnant the women and wine.

Yes we all know how it feels to cop a feel to get hit hard in the nuts we all know what the bitch needs and each masterpiece gives us more of a man's mind. We all know how it is to marry Hortense the radish or Cornish Hen (the chronic vaginismus, the menarche, the headache). You may grow fat and bald and tell whoopy poopy jew-by-the-john jokes but you are never the nagging wife of some such dream.

You always get the girl you never go back with the boyfriend who beat you.

You who twisted the necks of chickens wrote the modern picaresque novel looking through the peephole from the boy's lockerroom; wrote dirty limericks in ketchup on the pillowcase and committed copycat crimes; scrambled newsprint in small towns; plagiarized slapstick and stole the farts from louts who belch smoke drink cuss and gangbang; you spoke in triumphant monosyllables; I know you, you wrote History, parts I and II, spilling your guts on Ionic columns, you wrote *emu* and no one looked it up.

As each act begins my lips loll and loll around the edges of your marvelous instrument and each act ends with the pleasing spectre of cum on the face of the one you love. Do these whores do women do they?

I have gone beyond the parameter of your desire, I have found my own dense blue ache. The desire is amorphous and no amount of violence can subdue it. It liquefies and pools, the walls mulch and grind, long after the act is over.

In the glut bloat slouch of your unnecessary middle age I write with hoof pick and eye. I am the fat misanthrope in for my champagne brunch. I hope the adolescent knockwurst fits (no woman ever wrote no book like this no woman afraid

43

of being called ugly, bitch, foul-mouthed; ballbreaker, bad in bed, needs one thing).

You didn't think I could make a raft for my Tennessee slang or write about Dublin? You didn't think that I would speak to the man who spoke to my mother and not to me? You didn't think that I could drink the worm off the bottom of the bottle? Or catch the big fish all alone out at sea?

What makes you think the mindless vegetation have no feelings Emu, my man?

Now then. Do your itty bitty titties fit—the champagne glass? You will not get the job because I will sit before you, large and perspiring and schnauzer-nosed, asking how long you have sat in the harem and done each other's nails and hair (and if you are lucky you will be the one I choose to do my laundry and you will do it in your bikini briefs).

And when I go boxing off to war you can diet and file away your brain waiting for the fog horn and an impartial sea to announce my arrival home. I will leave my machete by the bed.

Are you pulling your dicks, you out there in the audience?

When the chaffinches fly off to the galápagos rift community you will stay in the gazebo, take your mudbaths in the antediluvian Mesopotamia and balance baskets full of birds on your head, walking back and forth to the Congo singing as the sun rises early each morning to do your wash. Nurturance, deference and passivity are endearing qualities in a man and your family will love you and Culture will put your face on vessels and let you live posthumously as art.

You will live theoretical and vicarious lives. Your doors will be opened. You will be fattened and then fucked.

You can vote and join a political party and you can frost your hair and stand by his side, a first lady, whimpering and bleating: don't kill the baby seals save the whales let us reimburse the indians. Perhaps you are the young nymphet page from Oklahoma assigned to one of the Redwoods in the senate, attached to his arm white and spindly under his dress shirt, working your way up. He says he can make you a congressperson some day; do you know how much sperm, oil, and Spam he owns on Capitol Hill, how many people he knows in institutions like Harvard, brothels, and the Pantheon; how many quack-footed conglomerates bobble when he talks, how many constituents get their due process from him how many bill of rights blacktie dinners he has attended before you baby baby do it and you're in (stop the burning brides in India, your voice trails off, *send dowries.*)

When you get there you will be seated up on the banquet table with an apple in your mouth until your escort arrives. Polygamy is practiced widely in this room. You are introduced as his wife but privately he tells you you can call him *daddy.* (we must pick the flies off starving children) But try as you may, you are no statesman in your toga. You are fierce in your lingerie. You are wicked and whisper.

The one who leads the senate subcommittee on racketeering, narcotics, gambling, and prostitution says *she's a pretty one where did you get her* (a carving in ice) you cannot stand such gratitude and before you can answer you have disappeared, a human puddle.

You jump out of the Trojan horse, a jew mother, telling its children to eat, eat.

The pinup girl on America's bunker they'll have you know is all belly breasts buttocks—a Paleolithic figurine— white meat—and you got all the overtime you'll ever need during the last war. When the surplus of children and weapons becomes a national problem at 65, you become America's mother, a rhombus subsidized by the State, taking long transverse walks and speaking of irregularity to someone who is frisky and losing his prostate.

You can always walk a little further, recoil or believe; say no.

The more corporate, academic and religious the men the more titillating and dangerous you become. It is the olive drab speaker speaking when a gravelly voice in a douche commercial alludes to your messy religious function and though you are pinched by a holy roller in a plaid suit you may retain this vote in absentia only. You may attend the next war providing you do not fight. Because you are not on the war poster they will be there to snap rubbers in your face and perform quick rude acts of raunch and bravado. Small boys will pop the maraschino cherry right out of your drink and belt your name out into a locker room where a covey of very critical and uncompromising sharp-billed geese, satirists, and self-indulgent types, await your anatomical monstrosities with every gaffe known to Freud.

You will not enjoy the malt liquor and you will make embarrassing demands on the supplies.

Stop the killing of girls in China (to get that only begotten son) *send boys.*

But Crawdad is there, again, to pick from his Cajun chicken the perfect teeth to draw from his festering cigar the encrusted lip; chafing and wheezing, old man holding his prostate, he serenades your demands—a slender tiparillo from across the room—with his moistened brown bankroll (he stole Helen of Troy and you alone could be the one he rolls off his jaunty presses with rolled-up sleeves to feed the boys serving their country from his desk).

Come out from behind your mousy brown eyes to watch the war, beautiful.

Give me your badge # you plead but all of Islam grins its five o'clock shadow.

Muhammad Senor Popadopalos Joe "The Boil"
Gaglianna Humbert Humbert or the Brontë Society, ju-
risprudence is his name. And he mentions with insouci-
ance and no malice whatsoever that he needs a mistress or
a masseuse.
Emily waiting alone in the attic with her peg board,
bears down on her Lexicon and sits up with her one thought
Erect.
You have your 3 canisters and your dog Keeper, your
cronies at Haworth, your red room, the family sitcom, death
and damnation—or this swanky sadsack hotel for glowing
ladies—he informs you—to the locomotive laughter of the
others.

You give to your one mulatto or mongoloid child, a
rhubarb to carry. Tell her to ignore the boys who only want
one thing: your analogous and miniature organs. She will
learn to love these men vicariously through women.

47

Killing the Shrimp

"She was not afraid of mice—"

It was the place I had in mind when I dug to China from a small glitch in the backyard. I appeared from under a table (still oozing the warm brown jism of earth) and there was a gingko tree, a fragrant waterfall and an ancient master tending his tiny perennials by the cash register. She was late again, but I had the whole Chinese zodiac to read, right there on my place mat.

The old man grows into himself like a bonsai, small and sturdy, practicing his martial arts on hypothetical assailants twice his size. Small children stop to ask him about his moustache and he can talk all day about his family and it will mean something. Conceived in silence, his daughter stands beside him like a kiwi fruit, and goes to seat the customers.

There we were, the four summers of my life, the two of us, grinning in apesuits. She, fortyish, funny, and still a girl. Each morning straight to the suntan bar for our salves, balms, ointments. Became wildly amorous taking our morning's whiff of tropical blend from the one bottle we found washed up on the beach; mango, aloe, paba, papaya, cocoa butter, coconut oil, almond, the goddess aphrodite. The drink smells real.

She started her days late, exasperated, sweating luxuriously. I waited for her to do my back. Some mornings I braved the chill and mesmerized by the ingots of the underwater—timelessness, its kryptonites and beams— looked up, to find her standing there on the one leg, some endangered beautiful bird, barebacked, in her strapless sarong. I told her to come on in (the water feeling fine) but she would not be ready until dusk and I would climb out, bittercold, histrionic, extending for the towel.

Dipping her hand into the goddess aphrodite et al., she passed her hand over the ribbing of my back until the snakespine glistened. Our skins were succulents. Slick and rich. The sun was sumptuous over the snakescape of our backs. I would pass my hand down the knots of her vertebrae, pausing over each hillock, and she would count the slow rolling knobs of the abacus as I passed over them. But time would not pass.

In walked Nora on her Bombay elephant, A Turk on a carpet, the Far East. She is let down slowly, evenly, in the curl of its trunk. She could have been an egyptologist or a queen, she wore a tiara and her hair piled high, around and around. She had the posture of a woman with a basket on her head, a long vulnerable neck and throat; the eyes of a cat: emerald, almond, green; trapezoid or yellow.

A one-dollar dress, she said, do you like it? I said I liked it and I did.

She hitched up her stockings to reveal the rest.

I gave myself a mohawk and looked stupid.

The chefs were Samurai and the waitresses were geisha types; they served us delicacies, butterflies and birds, and small flecks of color, with small preened hands, pouring out the tea and speaking only in haiku. Hearing the treble of her tiny constricted throat and then the coo coo, Nora turned and in a slack, warbling voice, ordered her vodka gimlet then changed her mind.

Have the gimlet, I told her, it's already made.

We were lifeguards and we owned the sun. The pool clear and blue as an emerald and the whole ocean behind the bathhouse. It was happy hour in the Tiki Room and already she was finishing my sentences.

Her hands poised around the teacup, accentuating the middle and index finger, a fish lipping water, she spoke, her mouth opening and closing like the rare gourami fish, each ecstasy a moment.

Each word removed from the graceful pulsing mouth like the one bead.

I remember the first time she said *fettucini alfrrredo.*

It was dusk and she was ready to dive in. We had dipped into our secret stash back at the bathhouse and we packed the old spitfire motor into the leaky dingy and paddled out to the Pit, we called it, where the sludge was so impossible and the vacuum so cumbersome and the pay so bad we overturned to play, fleshy sonar porpoises, bleating like babies, baa-ing like lambs, gliding through ring buoys and dredging into the bottom of the gruel for coins and bouillabaisse with the clump of our hands. We spooked and surfaced two at a time to cart wheel and cavort off the high dive: Nora and her A bomb impersonations and me and my terrible two-and-a-half.

For dinner she said, I'm having *fettucini alfrrredo.*

I'm buzzed she said and I was too.

She did it with James' squeaktoy when James wasn't looking. James her best friend, her dog. James' squeaktoy was surreal in bed. It was a hot dog on a half bun and she bought it for James' stocking for seventy-nine cents. What a bargain, I told her. With the price of produce these days, I'll switch to pet supplies. And what an Indian giver you are. And how disgusting, playing in all that doggy slime.

Dirty bitch.

My turn.

My night with Limbo in his bikini briefs. How good and how big. Go on she said. From Trinidad whose name I could not remember. Whose name I could not pronounce go on she said his hips gyrating to the floor of the Islander hotel

51

Portrait of a Girl

Hyannis barroom as sweaty and as homogenous as the beat of an erogenous banshi drum (you fifteen and as all-New England as the McIntosh apple—) she opened her legs just a crease— into the pelvic thrusts of the third world (nativity scene) she laughed, a nervous laugh—the sheer agony of it.

Our bowls of eggdrop soup.

The look of the latin lovers backed up against the underwater jets.

Then the loss of a creole jazzman incited our frantic imbibation.

She politely sipped the aperitif, a viscous bisque, as I descended my chopsticks into the soup.

I heard the slight smack of briny wetness and room was made for a small flambe.

Tearing texture from her bread she thanked the waitress in a kind and demure way. (So good with condiments, so good at splitting the seams of a papaya or a peach or pomegranate and drawing the exotic juices out onto the browning thigh, I asked her to please pass the bread.)

Looking at me with great compassion, trembling, she pressed it into my hand.

There was more to it than that (for I am a fine storyteller and this business of the silk dragon, it excites me).

My palms, sweating elegantly asked, who is this woman and why is she pressing the rhubarb into me with such compassion?

Again, I could not work my chopsticks fast enough into the crunch of the lonely wanton or nibble the spareribs down to the funk.

What makes a woman make love to her butterfly shrimp? Does she practice at sushi bars, on squid and octopus, nights, at home, alone, in front of the handmirror? One of those cans of oily imported fishes?

The shrimp are marvelous she said.
Difficult to fathom, I agreed.
You bitch. I have to pee. (She had what one would call a truly woman's rump. One side, then the other.)

Nora was elliptical in conversation like the waitress she would keep coming back with little flourishes and touches and whispers, here and there, a parasol for the drink, a flower for the hair, a slice of pineapple, and finger bowls, places for the eyes; like a babushka doll uncovering one dish after another, birthing each to each, abracadabra and voilá, and like the crunchy snow pea all for the moment's gustation.

Yes, miss, the soup could not gulp itself down fast enough. I know the Chinese are an unimpassioned people but we would like another round of drink. A ruby-throated hummingbird, she flies backward from the table.

The moment she switches to mai tai the night is on.

Nora looks down at her place mat and announces: You are *the*—you are the *dog*. Her tongue is thick swollen garlic orbs, congested mushrooms. She has trouble speaking. *Generous and loyal you have the ability to work well with others.*

Do you know what you are a cross between Liz Taylor Sylvia Plath Queen Nefertitty and a ca-cat.

You bitch she says. (I don't see a *cat*.)

No it says here that you are the *ra-rat. Ambitious and sincere you can be generous with your financial resources.*

You bitch she says, I'm not the rat and *you* can get the check.

The dog does not love the one who pays for her food. The dog loves the one who feeds her face.

She spoke sensuous Spanish she got that way on booze, curled her tongue with the elegant charm of the islands, magic snake tongue, as we rattled back and forth like

moroccos, doing the cha-cha. She had a marimba on her
mantel and sometimes we played.

Don Wong at the bar with a shrunken head and a thatch
of hair likes shit-faced ornithischians, I told her. Over
there by the botanical gardens.

When she sees him she says oh la la, créme de la créme.

You are old enough to be its mother.

You bitch.

Where did she learn to make the shrimp writhe? I
suddenly do not know what country we are in; gone is the
undulating flame from our volatile cuisine.

After we individually palpate each zone of the tongue,
its swells and buds and involutions, we work the taste into
our mouths, another day to remember, and she arrives, the
exquisite sweetness of almond or macaroon.

We get our warm moist finger lozenges and mandarin
oranges. Bloated like anemone, we spackle our impacted
faces, not ostensibly, as we had wished. Asking for a doggy
bag.

Jaded; surfeit and excess. Lotus; indolence and dreamy
contentment. Fleshy, fragrant smelling engorged. Feeling
fine and female.

She left lipstick kisses on her orange skins, a pair of
magenta moans. Her blotting paper everywhere.

They will put me in the fat farm she said.

The waitress hands me the tarotpack.

let's go Nora her bobtail leads the way we can fly like
them multicolored kontiki birds sing ling ding too muchy
mai tai too muchy barrels molded ribbed coconut for the
pleasure of the lady shrimps languorously apprehended in
the Tiki Room was it I kept saying take your shoes off and

we did sweet and sour feet all those red exotic chinadolls
birddragons firebreathing Don Wong at the bar panning
for fossils chimes chinkling my temples pelting sing ling
ding tingling then us tinkling our tuning forks on teacups
a lipstick kiss on origami napkin fish and birds fortune
cookies and yes yes we exchanged parasols mine popped
a sprocket she carried it out in her teeth and me in the
spaghetti skins of my poptop all eyes on her Carmen and
her castanets lipping goodbye to the jolly Chinese to Won
the waiter sayonara get some sun go walk your fu manchu
mr. year of the dog the yin and yang of the family business
keep the yen
    The one about one hung lo, then where.
    The ocean in my ears. Her place. Head hung lo. My god
the rug. woe and woe and woe she said *villa* she said *bistro*
she said *bungalow* takes her bath in a bubbling chablis
what is it she does in the white porcelain tub with pouches
of pinescent and conifer rattan furniture a wickerbasket
by the tub: pumice stone coral shell loofa loofa scented
soap smell of honeybee what's in here must be nectar pink
vanity chair by the toilet an overturned handmirror my
lazy laughing eyes what for do the sylphs do her hair that
frazzled jet black Clairol color working their little squeeze
bottles boudoir heaven do the dolphins do her eyes the
melting blue grey birds at the breakfast table I imagine
small elves butter her toast but when the mirror is held up
she laughs at the bouncy banana curls and three kinds of
doves fly out of her expletives
    I'm up here I said (boudoir heaven) I'll be down.
    too muchy mai tai
    my too muchy solly
    mad about the rug? I've spoiled my pinafore. I can't
hold back my rrr's. I can't stop my rrr's from rolling. (it
comes at you Kong upside down bigger than the Whale

Portrait of a Girl

tickling your throat with a hairy finger heave ho your guts
into the canopic jar call me Ishmael I'm almost done)

When the kitty shat on the Oriental remnant by the fire
the kitty was picked up by the neck of the napehair and
stuck into his naughty kitty litty box. Rowr.

I'm up here I'll be down give me time to think up here
on the toilette a head in its hands the wooly mammoth no
pretty sight why not windchimes for the linen closet a
chandelier tinkle tinkle for toity an icebucket for my head
what's this a goddamned fresco for the bed and bath each
tile a story of its own I see an Egyptian with boxed hands
did you have the aztecs in to perform their trigonometric
functions on the tile

my god the rug

what did I tell her about time dilation hoof and pick
iconography eye the two of us grinning in apesuits a year
in space is a year off your face Einstein theory of relativity
length contraction the yin yang shorter moving faster into
you yes I say to use my example my prowess with
mnemonics my hippocampus I will be Bucksy Mulligan
the ornery medical student someday I will what's your
favorite hormone Nora that's what I said Oxytocin the
answer I tell her to whom we owe the Big O shotguns
flushes bombs babies also up in our crow's nest perch
swinging the Acme Thunderer now Nora we drunk our
snotgreen sea our ivory tower I steal my dreams from you
we can fly like them multicolored kontiki birds our version
of the snotgreen sea Nora Joyce who said it read books get
out of bed what's this I say Pprrpffrrppfff plagiarism of
the Joycean ending bitter satire of a stinking stream of
consciousness bean sculpture fart she says it's OK end
of my youth last summer of my life cha cha cha and cha
cha cha Nora do you get it I'm laughing she says

do you take your bath in sparkling pisswater you sleep with that dog's plaything your loofa is like leather I cannot eat it I've seen those sweaty gouges on your terrified nose from the bridge of your gaudy glasses the ones junked in a wickerbasket on the counter by the checkout with the toenail clippers and the ten cent pocket combs somebody already ran through his hair some third world Dong Wong in his tacky Bermuda chest when you stand up you have one sticky venetian blind behind and roll your rrr's one then the other for every Carlos with no teeth who wants some instamatic piece of ass pick up your orange peels miss avant garde miss one dollar dress do you import your breath certain spices from the far east hymen from China where do you keep your Bombay elephant say bung-a-hole fettucini my asso do you speak Spanish Sahara do you

your mouth is a pawnshop I am the mycologist mushroom lover lover of words your rare finds your what nots your verbs blush your nouns moan the woman herself can't spell Nora and that is gratifying too

Answer the question Nora
go get your knife
and your bag lunch.

I hear the almighty ocean in my ears head hung lo again the white angora rug from Woolco I don't fool all pinky syrupy goostick of grenadine—now about that claret—I have had a problem with the lobster bisque Madame forgive me in the lavatoire the newburg sauce imagine all of Egypt looking on when you whisk me out like the Beelzebub at five a.m. I say Rowr you can't do this to me Nora the diminutive of Eleanor go back and pick you pussens by the napehair mafia princess here here's the handmirror geisha girl go fuck the tourists with your classical arts I so solly I spoiled the tapestry Ichikoo off off with you you are like clams marsala you are gritty down

there I'll get back to you in later life femme fatale I'm in love
with you too

(so beautiful and never getting out of bed except for the
chamberpot or the handmirror molly you're killing the
shrimp)

And when the bottle washes up on the beach I order the
usual thick dark rich Adonis with oily abs well hung and I
take the genie with her three breathy wishes too

and my heart beats on forever young, Sub gum, Sub
gum.

Flour, Sugar, Water

"she loved winter, snow, and ice.
(They went home and broke their bread
brushed their teeth
and went to bed.)"

From the vents of the sulfide hot springs, with the clams, crabs, mussels, worms, barnacles, whelks, leeches, and limpets, I emerged, spreading the eelgrass from my eyes and I did them like they did me. Wrote treacherous articles for the school newspaper (eat shit, motherfucker).

I was at that most prestigious institution second oldest after Harvard, the college of—

We didn't go to class, we hunted down the ghetto prophets cuz the goddamned southern baptist pimps got to us. *Dog is to hydrant as whore is to lamppost.* Women embellish the children excel the men provide. (We laughed right into that ho's foreign little crack of a face.)

the city was lit me and tjossie we was living in our skins we made the clerk load the vibrators the ones with all the tenebrous feelers sat in on one reel of Debbie Does Dallas with two sailors one who said kiss it one who had tattoos and bad teeth

We were the life of the party. The gumball's nose. The grinning grin. It caused some people palpable pain. Like any college coed we kept pumping beer for the boys hooked to our arms who said we was beautiful.

the sailors said so long isodora so long jezebel we said so long sailors

We flew home Christmas, summers, and when our grandfathers died.

We jumped from too high into our aboveground pools and kissed too passionately on the hug 'n' swing. We ventured outside the ABO blood system without an ambulance or a driver and took everything pass-fail.

We piled into the orange mgb—cockroaches, party animals, caped crusaders—speeding toward necropolis *scrunch and die scrunch and die* (go gamma phi); the secret pulsing handshake, a phonebooth full of drunken pledges; memoirs of a lost life. (It is improbable that we grow old or hungry here.)

When I learned that William F. Buckley was to give the valedictory address I knew I was had. He had the parents unilateral support and the alumni swooning.

I was not a Rhodes scholar. I would never be that clean. And I would flunk the placement test to avoid them and cry all night about my broken dreams. Imagining him there at the podium I tightened my sphincter muscles and stopped what I was thinking. I made a citizen's arrest. I did not want him there on my big day.

He will not address a predominantly black audience or tell them he could probably get used to kinky hair if he himself had it. That he has sometimes wondered, but not for long. He will not confess that he finds himself quite knowledgeable, but never absolute; that he has never really understood the atom, or cared to read *Ulysses*.

He will not make enemies to tell the truth or admit that he has lied to feel good. He will not have to admit that he has willingly answered a question wrong on a multiple choice test or scored his own exam. He will not say: I do not have herpes and I am secretly proud.

He will not want emancipation or plead for another amendment.
He will not fall down off a chugging pyramid to break his leg.
He will not know I am here.
He will not frisk the papacy for signs of life.
(I sometimes lay awake, Consuela of Dublin, mother of the novel, I speak no english I'm being very *candida* I have no award my husband he is yes please thank you very much I would like to say something but all I could do is heckle and blow kisses having wasted my parents money and alumni dreams making up my mind about the gpa.)
When I reap the conference of my honorary degree I pack the ovations and stand to tell them: We must carry Truth everywhere, beyond the human absorption spectrum and behind the ears, and we shall climb to the stars, necessary and evil, and at an oblique angle, wanting to go home, spitting on ourselves and others to neutralize our fears and prejudices, to learn to love ourselves. We shall never apologize to our domestic enemies for having done the good of all mankind!
The pop of a frothing lukewarm champagne marked the wings of our nirvana and our dreams imbued our lives with rich and dangerous substances. We would arrive, somehow, without strategies or skills; our futures together secure as seen from the chugging pyramid of our long summers; though things at home were changing.
When we were called upon to roll the meatballs, set the table, or say the homily, we sacrificed our disrespect, our recklessness and imagination, and lopped off an ear.

The snow bled into the drifts unnoticed; he was hard to get to know. Mother scolded him, not ungraciously but with equanimity, like she scolded the dog who chose his moments injudiciously or licked her knives, forks, and children; he like the rancid dishrag sat too long; the turkey gizzard, the giblet organ she pulled sopping and offensive from the family bird every Thanksgiving and he was no bargain at 165 lbs. of gristle and bone.

Her in-laws sat five years in the upstairs of the doctor's home, breathing each other's innards like wastes. Nobody's fault. Sat like two bickering maids, curling into the uncomfortable anticlimax of the son's home. The one jibbering away, the other, waiting for his time to talk. The mutt and jeff of dying. The mutt and jeff of dreams. Each dreaming the other's dream.

They should have punched off into the air with the shuttlecocks, sat in the cabana at West Palm beach, and with the swift clean click of the mallet played that last leisurely game of croquet.

He was the mongoloid child she bore unwittingly after 40 (an abject cruelty, a virgin birth).

We always had a soup spoon, a butter knife, a salad fork and we always ate the aperitif, the entrée, and then dessert. Morality was a simple matter of eating what was on the plate, clearing our deadwood, and holding up our cards. Staying alive meant not bringing mayonnaise to school, not coming out of swim team with wet hair, leaving stray birdfeathers alone and staying away from the deepfat fryer. We had our pleasures, too: alphabet soup, a few jimmies, silver beads and red hots, one lick at the spoon each; sillyputty allowed in the one room.

He could have been one of her clodhoppers, one of her doodly-poopers, too; her household pest, another mop of hair, a tousled head; she could have left the spaghetti pan by his bed, his vermin emptied lovingly with the pastina like ours; she might have said higgledy piggledy, this pig, that pig; but something went malignant: time. One lung. Ten kinds of cancer, all grown from innocent moles. He had outgrown the mark on the wall.

Otherwise, everything was fine; she might have shooed him off no further than Osh Kosh Timbuktu the moon or out of her hair.

She always knew when it was time; time to get up, time for school, time to carve the smiling face on the jack-o-lantern, time to hang the on-again-off-again blinking lights; time for the family trip to the turkey farm, time to make and confirm the reservation; time to clean the silverware drawer; gold silver or bronze she knew what anniversary it was; when it was time to make styrofoam Christmas ornaments, time to be good, time to frost the cake and lick the spoon; time for puff balls and cocoons; time to get our pajamas on, time to empty the lint from the dryer, time to say good-bye; set the clocks ahead or behind one hour time to hide and dye the eggs and when the shirttails were ready for March winds, she said, it was *his time to go.*

When the skee balls came rattling out of the gutter of the clown's face at fun-o-rama, she was behind you, aiming her shot, and when, at Plymouth Rock, the candle was about to be dipped or the shot fired, she looked at it and then at us, a smoking musket, camera ready (did you see it kids).

She knew which crayon was missing and she knew who left the faucet running and for how long. No bones about it.

She knew because she could spell forsythia and chrysanthemum could spell pasketti or spaghetti and because she knew every s in Mississippi, four in all, could pick a peck of pickled peppers and always saw the llama first. She called it the king's English but when she pulled it from the family bird it became the pope's tail or horse's ass.

We used jelly jars as drinking glasses and on the bottom of each one was a different member of the Flintstone family.

She got out the extra leaf for the dining room table and enlisted my help, pushing from the other end. We removed the storm windows (this side up). She called me Maybelle, my name when I helped around the house, and Maybelle got the guest towels out, the embroidered ones with the Initials. She reminded me to dust the legs of the coffee table and there was something I forgot to do in the blue bathroom. She rolled out the muslin fabric and we cloaked the table. The longest word in the English language is antidisestablishmentarianism. I did not have to put the napkins and silverware where they belonged because it was après-wake with a light buffet and things did not have to go where they had to. We would use paper products that day.

At all these necessary affairs she took out the spaghetti pan for throw-up. This time to boil noodles in.

That morning I scalded the milk, scratched the teflon, sucked up paper clips and small change with the vacuum cleaner; on hardwood floors I did not switch to the downy brush and she told me my fingers smelled like they shouldn't. I fluffed the centerpiece; it was brittle and shed; I left the two pennies in the dryer to rattle with his eyes. (I always let the pumpkin sit too long; I kept the wreath up until I splintered my stockinged feet with the ghost-white spindles.) She always had the boxes marked XMAS away before New Year's. I jump up and down until the cake falls.

It was his time to go, and he was a fussy eater, I know.

I have trouble adjusting to the pluperfect past.

I am a cranky child and nothing pleases me. If my dress is wrinkly I will throw it away, or wear it, as is.

We are all called upon to make carnations out of tissues in later life. We sat there, tying rags to the tails of begotten kites, dipping eggs, carving doilies, cutting rows and rows of stalactite teeth into the ghastly lace. Sent out to the front lawn to look for another centerpiece, I gripe, return with macabre goodies and games of chance, party favors for the distinguished guests; I have no abilities when it comes to day-to-day living. (She was not beyond stopping the station wagon dead in its tracks and throwing the dog into the front seat to collect her pussywillows or the one cat-o-nine.)

I do a clog dance because the tulips are coming; the cars stop to look at me. Where to today? One wants to play scrabble, one wants to see Santa, one wants blueberry picking, one begs for the Blue Angels but only one has her heart set on the turkey farm.

She was wearing her lei and it was a kind of family powwow. Sometimes we swallowed the gourds on Halloween like after-dinner mints.

But when it was my turn to lick the frosting from the spoon, I ran. She dispensed the prizes from the cereal box equitably and knew before we even asked.

She poured baconfat into the same shotglass on the bottom shelf of the buzzing frigidaire her whole married life and was accused of massmindedness by my generation. It was true she kept some old tins of cloves and currents that could haunt a shelf. But when it was time—the milk passé or a creditor past due—she moved the reconstituted lemon juice and found the spices to fumigate the wreath.

For she who shucks the corn and snaps the beans, time does not pass.

Because of her, each of us can tell time and tie his or her own shoe.

She held my hand until the grass fire was out and after an afternoon of breading and frying when her hands were incapacitated with flour sugar water, things measured and presumed, I finished her sentences. She who knew the poisons sumac and ivy, the dippers, big from little, the hurricanes Abigail and Ann, knew her goblets, water from wine; she who said achoo bless you, gesundheit—the only German—she ever spoke—she knew—her perishables and perennials and always cut along the perforation point opened the box this side up bronzed each baby shoe handed me the silver spoons for when my sublime abstract world went kaput. She always held a row of straight pins on her lower lip. She scratched her scalp with her darning needle and tracked hurricanes with her divining stick. All of her degrees were conferred on us, but it was she who sat on her progeny, keeping it human; it was she who in the unutterable silences of my childhood taught me the oriental arts, knew I liked white meat, knew when the pineapple was ripe.

She who knew how many and how long she who told us are we there yet; she who washed our hair in the kitchen sink knew how many cards in a penochle deck; was incahoots with god, had a tea kettle that called to her and her only; fed us her chapsticks, her breathmints, fish on Friday; changed our sheets on Monday and left five ripening tomatoes on the windowsill; she who explained the firefly explained Hiroshima, the sonic boom; she who separated whites from darks, knew the aesthetics of egg yellows and egg whites, could remove the static cling from cob webs, always found the odd sock.

Every Fall I wait for her, for my lunchbox, my pencil box, and my three bargain dresses. She is my mother. She wears girdles, earrings, high heels, and hot wax. But in a detached and perfunctory way.

In a cashmere coat mother looked a bit uncomfortable, like she was missing one of her kids.

At 21 she still spotcleaned my dress, licked and patted down my cowlick with her two fingers. I still go to her to hear the things I already know.

She sells seashells by the seashore but her palindromes are autocratic and preemptive. They save me from the terminus at either end.

She left me alone in the bathtub for two seconds and I wrote *Mein Kampf.* When I reach the void at the end of the word, I still strive. (the rest is history)

I asked her, mother, did the groundhog see his shadow today? She shook the light bulb, caught the rattle of the dead filament, tousled my head, added the basil leaf to the simmering sauce; I waited for her trained ear, and the thermometer popped out of the family bird.

She watched while we played Marco Polo, heard our kites on the ground; knew when, with all our various little legs, we could not push the swing.

How could I ever sufficiently love, the woman who had packed for the whole family that rainy day.

(She did not have me on hunches and hindsight alone.)

? may a moody baby doom a yam ?

Inspector #3

"Madeline woke up two hours
later, in a room with flowers."

We were ushered into a stretch limousine and the lurch
in the monkeysuit and the three-pronged candelabra lit our
way to the funeral home. The cars let us pass.
(he took us out after dinner to dairy freeze and nana
would say Winthrop! and we loved it when she said
Winthrop! and that funny upside down moment—fast then
faster—over the hills Winthrop! and I grew older and I
never let him suffer that terrible indignity I kept saying yes
faster yet! still! Winthrop!)
Mind your p's and q's Winthrop. (That last night at
dinner we all whispered to ourselves: I hope the coachman
gets us to your destination before you start to smell. But we
were too ashamed to listen.)
Mother tells us we are here.
The lurch lets the cookie lady of Rumford Maine out of
the stretch limousine. She felt woozy she wobbled she wore
soft shoes call cobbies; the hunchback Igor with his ob-
scenely large latchkey will now open officially the clunky
gates of Christiandom, moonlighting as his living room,
and we must kneel, in turn, before a body, killed twice, and
pray.
Father hands over the family coats. Mother's pocketbook matches her shoes.
Garish old man, we have put your orange wig on a stand
and now we know.
Your little lady, your surviving wife, the Mrs. T, looks
a little annoyed or a little confused as she screws down her

face into your plexiglass stare; her argumentative and
bungled mind asking what ails you anyway (I've lost my
glasses I've lost my bag). She did not know who you
pretended to be, all gussied up, a macaroon or a miniature
poodle, and what the fuss was all about, and she cried softly
and sweetly and to herself and I felt sick to my stomach and
I knew that when she came to me in her spotty navy blue
dress and some blip of paper with Inspector #3 on it Mae
Mae Mae what's it say I would have to tell her it is the place
where he snowshoed in Maine as a boy the walls of the cabin
are smoked knotwood pine and she inhales the whole ten
acres intrinsically in one breath. Yes, I told her, that's what
it says, the dogs enjoyed each other, that was enough; just
the two of you, the his and her, the Mr. and Mrs. T.

I held my fingers up, I pulled apart the clutter of her
mind, I held up the soft webbed threads of her neuroglia,
the flotsam and the jetsam of her mind, in the pads of my
fingers and we played cat's cradle; they were slightly sticky,
the effluvia of her wispy and discordant thoughts, like the
hairnets she floated in around the house. She had that look
on her face again (Winthrop where's your nitroglycerine);
she was going to stuff the bread in the scissor drawer; the
spring sprung back at my hand from her soft larval existence, and she teeter-tottered over to her seat, knotting
together her rosary with pink gnarled hands, burbling like
a baby, while I marvelled at her gentleness with god.
Winthrop's having his nap, I told her.

Winthrop's having his nap.

I watched the others, wondered what they extracted
from the unknown, from raindance or ritual, from wormy
doom.

I lay the carnation on him, on his stiff clasped hands.
What to say, RIP, the lord be with you, too; mutter a few

offhand prayers dilate the room's shrouded personnae; but like the mantis praying, I am really eating.

I am like you nana. I have forgotten what I was to remember.

Your husband, my grandfather, Harry Hope, gin bear, buried alive today with his booze and pipe dreams.

I said two hail marys full of grace the lord is with thee one quick rudimentary our father who art in heaven but all I could see was her, out of the corner of my eye, sick with heat, all balled up, knotting her kleenex into a rosary, burbling, again. I wanted her to press against me with the soft hot crush of her face and cherish the eternity before she wiped the lipstick off my face. I wanted her to squeeze my face when she kissed me. I wanted to hold her until she was no longer human. I guess I always knew she would die, a bird swooping into the glass. The windshield of a compact car.

That I would be left holding her plastic statue of St. Jude.

I who caught her gobbling bonbons now and again little lady as fast as they fall putting them back, too blind to see, the fissures oozing the odious and much maligned raspberry goo; I caught her hot hand in the box full of the indescribable delectables, time and time again, the ineluctable unmentionables, the secret centers. I did not tell. She had every right to her sublime.

I knew when she sneaked a smoke up in the blue bathroom, that she hoarded her chocolate bars in her nightdress and soaked her underpants at 4:00 when mother watched Wheel of Fortune.

In a rare public moment we bought caramel corn and stuffed our gassing spewing selves into the photo booth at the five and dime and we bought queen-size hose with a seam, hairnets, rubberbands and paperclips, and we looked everywhere for penuche fudge and she gave me a little something for myself.

Her charge cards were spilling all over the mall and every ten feet we counted her money.

I was hooked to her arm and she called me lady, little lady, lady godiva, or lady jane, and I knew I belonged to her, because when she recognized something dear or familiar she would say it in a simpering singsong voice, like it was hers, *cat-o-nine*, like she had grown it out back under her clothesline and that all others had sprung from that, and it was always *your* fiddle your *brother's* bugle *your* father *our* foolishness, *my* housecoat, and that's how she said it, *my* lady jane; ayap, ayap, aya, by and by, and just the same.

She was afraid to take the escalator so we had to catch the cargo elevator up from gift wrapping and she was afraid to get in so we checked to see if her glasses were in her pocketbook and they were.

I don't know that she had ideas, exactly, in later life but she got by on her opinions.

What were the mitigating factors of your smalltown grammarians, little lady, who taught you such diminutive nouns, few verbs, so many adjectives, the overwrought silences and punctuation, what went on at the mill? Who kept your softlead pencil point from the arch quadrants of the noun-verb-predicate world, the male world, and forced you to be the example, the cookie lady of Rumford Maine?

She thought the clerk owned the store and she offered her chiclets and peppermints.

She had a white house and a white car and a window box of red geraniums and she had an old-fashioned way of noticing when you had color in your cheeks.

She was not like me.

She was never in stirrups.

She was the grandmother who pointed to her ailments on the anatomical puppet.

She thought it was something that I was a woman's libber and I thought it was something that she had a plastic statue of St. Jude. But mostly she wanted to know when I'd be coming home again. She kept a roll of my letters in a rubber band and a flashlight by the bed and together we languished behind and between words.

There were things she'd justasoon not know and she complained only to Winthrop of the draft in the shed.

If there is a hermaphrodite in the receiving line, I am it. She drank from a checkerboard mug embossed with my name and she insisted. She loved me unequivocably and regardless and for myself.

I wanted to hold those hands warm and soft as muffins; she is my nana I goosed her in the beamend, I took her to the picture show, I signed my letters XXO; she's my pet nana she eats creamed corn and lima beans out of my napkin under the table.

It is her widow's debut.

She contends her mother named her Edwina by mistake. She will not answer to Edwina. She is very particulate about that.

We must take the bread out of the scissor drawer and begin. The company has begun to pay their respects. We must stand here, Edwina, somehow necessary, like the basket of fruit, the contribution to the American Cancer Society, the Hallmark card. You must remind Winthrop to clasp his hands demurelike, for he is dead.

Winthrop, if you could change back into your pajamas, you would. They have pinned you with the crawling boutonniere that only means one thing. (I want to see the rearing head, the one iguana. I want to see the inside mash, the gravy and giblet organs; I want to smell the funny smell.) Turn up your hearing aid, Winthrop, and hear the cicadas sing. It's time to count the legs on the centipede. It's time to turn back the bug. (The place is crawling with the Bloomsday newts and you have your own two bodyguards.)

Who will be here next Christmas, puppa, to bring your Johnnie Walker Red to the cardiologist, the internist, and the dambed-bejesus eyedoctor. Who will shoo the squirrels and pigeons off the feeder, who will poke at the fire and who will care about the rhododendrons and who will wait for the paper and the mail and who will rock the upstairs of the doctor's home and who will be scolded for shovelling snow with his heart condition and tipping the barrels in the garage with that eight cylinder boat of his and who will wear as his aftershave the deciduous musk of the forest, the Rumford Paper Company, and who will be in oblivion upstairs when Winthrop has had a few too many and who will take long walks up and down the driveway and who will die each summer lugging my suitcase to the car and who will thank me for the butane lighter and the electric shoeshine kit at Christmas, who will give his permission to wear the navy blue dress and who will cash your pension check on the fifth of the month who will wear your checkerboard cap who will boot me in the arse going upstairs who will finally tame the Androscoggin and who will be the last man alive to say *how do you do* and who will know the blizzards by the boot and who will listen to your wife tapping doodah, doodah, on the tabletops who will turn off the buzzing gizmo in your ear and who will know the indians and who will smell like Old Man of the Mountain, the Kennebec and Franconia Notch.

(As a child I saw you angling at Winnepausaukee and I thought that you were not a man but a profile of a grandfather.)

That last night at dinner we all found you secretly repugnant and scrambled for our respective chairs (the past, the horrible game of musical chairs). Nana said I think Winthrop's gone a little cuckoo; mother said he's flipped his lid; father said the cancer's reached his brain and we all asked, although we knew, what's wrong with puppa, but not before the echo answered—Winthrop, what's ailing you?

Your time had come, you always said, slower than molasses and just as welcome as the flowers in May. You died on Bloomsday and I knew you would. With a pocketful of scotchies, one son fine and lovely grandchildren a pipe and a wife. A pipe cleaner and a daughter-in-law who went through your tacklebox and discovered secretly that you could hear.

That's what this mass is all about.

The ten kinds of cancer all grown from innocent moles.

Your last fourteen nights strapped to the bed, mitts and all, wheezing your whole life's story in one inarticulate plea for air.

I could not lean over and kiss you (I was too scared).

You yanked your catheter out, spilled your last bag of piss. Last day I saw you they pulled out your false teeth and your whole mouth puckered and collapsed. I leaned over to kiss you and left the room; it seemed the noble thing to do.

But I can tell you now, granddaddy. This is your story. How the cafeteria girls dumped off your tray at noon and picked up your lunch at one. They never let you out of your mitts. How long had they left those lunches out of reach, on your bedside table.

And charged you for those meals (we could only whisper).

Nana kept saying Winthrop! and asking the doctor when you would *come to* (just where do you think *you're* going). (Her glare lingered on him long after the question until he forced her to say it again Winthrop! It behooved him to answer, but this one time she seemed to understand his insolence and by avoiding certain subjects, arrived at the truth.)

They tagged your right toe while we were in the next room, wondering what to feel, how to swallow. They sent your cane home, your old leather scuffies, your Old Spice, your shaving kit, your wife.

They're still in your room.

I breathe the unexpurgated musk of your prose, I confiscate all you owned in your pockets and pouches, under the floorboards, tell how time has ruined everything, how all the old times seemed like lies like they had never happened but in the wishful weary eyes of an old man, short of breath, idling on one lung. I am your underdog granddaughter, the family fun; your subterraneal crotchety ecstasies my favorite stories, too. I gather firewood to walk the dog and off the wharf of Winnipesaukee my sinker plummets into the embattered lives of the fishes. And I know that like a slow tortoise you head back to the Galapagos for good, to play a slow poking game of cribbage with your cronies back at the mill, still spiting your mother-in-law for seeing you like that, propped up, staring, your lies only half-understood.

I cast your shadow, trolling, back over the lake. Everything will be all right.

There is a morose lurch loitering in the back of the parlor waiting to be fed (he owns the joint—he embalms us all, and for a certain fee). He will drive us all in highfalutin style to a church.

And like the little von trapp family we are herded offstage one by one by our boxed ears by the Nazis clapping in the front row.

76

The consumptive chamber music begins, a covey of recalcitrant and jealous violins our cue, and a singing governess, as well; off to the calliope and we shall see: who will cry and who will carry on.

The Sisters Almeda and Alfreda

"To the tiger in the zoo
Madeline just said, 'Pooh-pooh,'
(Everybody had to cry—
not a single eye was dry.)"

We're here.

They sing of your murder in the mezzanine and although they sing hosanna in the highest nowhere can I find a description of your small perfect life together.

The chantreuse in the mezzanine who thinks she knew you, the choirs and the archangels on high, drag the air-conditioned goldfish baths for the glint of your satisfied remains, but there is no one here to represent the Rumford Paper Company and it was three years before you turned in those good ol' state-a-maine plates.

Burbling again, the baby. She always spoke of your death but she had a slow shuffle that allowed me to escape in time. But this is not her story.

When you leaned back, magnanimous, a kind of king of the old haunts, you had a story to tell and in a rare and exquisite moment before you spoke you lit the fire and fed the dog and emptied your pockets out onto the table while she tapped doodah, doodah on the tabletops you'd go on and on about the one room schoolmarm and every time you put the snake in the shoe she'd say Winthrop! Hush you ol' goat geezer you ol' gallant.

Does the priest here conducting your death have any mortal idea whatsoever how annoyed disgruntled you were with god; was it indifference you were feigning those fifty odd years playing putt putt golf strolling in and out of the haberdashery shining up your wing-tipped shoes and hanging out at the filling station half-hoping to find the castanets in the woodpile or see a naked lady.

As sure as the book is under the mattress and the key is in the mailbox, they ate at the Chuckwagon restaurant downtown ordering sirloin steaks medium well, just to be sure, and reviewing the menu every Saturday night as if to remind themselves of a choice they had to make.

She would say Winthrop! and he would move further into the booth.

There was a steer over the men's room and a cow with some flower garbage in her hair over mine (a bow or something, and of course a bell). I was the first grandchild of Rumford Maine to get so miffed I held it until I got home and they came at me all night, why I hadn't and what was wrong, each word exacerbating the next, because I couldn't tell them: they kept dumping their cooked apples on my plate long after I stopped liking them. In a cow and steer world I was an anomaly.

The garnish I ate off the sides of the plate was just a phase, too.

They never argued up front or discussed money, they bickered behind doors and feuds were built on the catches of conversation insinuated or overheard. When they quarrelled there was never anything at stake, really. As she got older she got more and more ferocious behind the waitress' back. She always got a lobster bib and later when she would forget to ask I would tell her that the waitress forgot her lobster bib.

And in some other life she was the stubborn elderly grandmother who stooped at town hall to take the first black drink.

They had their particular waitress and when she earned it Winthrop figured out her 15% and pressed it into the palm of her hand. This is how they felt about god and they had a right to their salvation downtown every Saturday night, sitting at a reserved table in the back of a converted conestoga caboose.

Winthrop? Did you give it to her? Winthrop! The *tip*.

We marched in, sat in the family pew, but I stood at the back of the church, barefoot in my gunnysack. I did not belong. I who loved you best, or in my own way. It was not my idea or theirs to cart you off in a stretch limousine, some lurch in a monkeysuit at the wheel, the mourners in for petits fours after mass. The cookie lady of Rumford Maine did not know she married such royalty, either.

(She only ever shuffled past the nightlight into the bathroom.)

But I knew the newt under the butter plate was you; and I knew it was you, puppa, at the wake of my granddaddy, who blew back into my ear, "He looks well." You sounded like one of the great aunts.

All around me I saw holy objects, and I froze: leather, rings, fishnets, veils, girdles, rubber lips, harness, heels and hot wax. (I'm not wearing no bell on no neck) (who kisses the cross kisses the shoe)

I wasn't allowed up there, in the sacristy, as a girl, except to vacuum and dust at six a.m. before mass and before I was even *up* and the way the priest had spoken that word *sacristy* I knew it was the place where men played poker and rolled the everlasting die at night and perhaps the room where I had been, by myself, frightened and alone, when my brother had whispered *murder* and laughed and told me that Madame Curie was the only female scientist *ever* and that she had discovered mold by *accident* and with

another *man* and that even all the good *chefs* were men and
that god *himself* was a *man.*

I believed this for an instant or for awhile or the way I
believed his finger when he licked it and went to check the
weather; I never believed it (but I think he did).

And I knew they spoke about the devil like a coed
restroom and this was the way they would speak about me.
Because it was the privileged place a man went to defecate,
flagellate, paddle, or talk babytalk, and it seemed to be the
women who were most at stake.

I never liked standing behind the dotted line. Or the
velvet roped-off section behind which those of the XX
chromosome could not pass. (I think I should know if the
anthropologists are excavating for skulls in my own church;
if the cops are chalking a silhouette around a murder
victim, it they are having sex in the ice cubes, or if the
neighbors are having a block party. I should like to know
if in the sacristy is another unsigned document from god; a
safe deposit box for evangelical sperm, little lambkins,
virgin births, non sequiturs. I should like to know if that is
where they keep the wives and children, if that is where
Hester Prynne was taught the one letter Alphabet, or if
that is were the sisters of mercy keep the woodplank leg.)

He stands up on the altar like a mandrill, his male
markings, his ecclesiastical warpaint, all over his face;
calls himself both man and mankind. (And who is to keep
the little girls from doing penance from finally looking up—
at christ's codpiece, sancrosanct and so big?) It is true that
before I cracked from rib of adam I was Woe of man and that
makes the whole story slightly suspicious (and monkeys,
too). You should forget about that great good indisputable
black book and bury my granddaddy, Father; rewrite the
dictionary; it preceded you. (I don't like the part where
Paul, a gentle man and a Christian (a man already in

82

quotes), says to his corinthians, "And don't let no woman make no man eat no vending machine munchies no microwave ham 'n' cheese.")

What bothers me most is the vulgarity of your civil remarks and the statistical abomination of domestic violence (crimes against wives) and (bah! yes! leading cause of death!) and the proven culpability of the male head-of-household (and to combat the advent of battery and rape the gospel says to avoid the mean-spirited husband and if he calls you stupid, why *shut up*:

"Wives should be submissive to their husbands as though to the Lord; because the husband is the head of the wife just as Christ is the head of the Church."

Around the poles of Merrymount I dance: heel come sit shit do it with savvy grace and tit. Tongues of flame! Tongues of flame!

Glick! Blee! (hit him back) (throw the ball stupid)

All the groaning banalities in the bible would make god, at the very least, a very poor writer. It behooves me to think that god is a better writer than I am. I hate to think that my soul, too, could be wrenched from me by another hoarde of ignominious young boys coming of age for the umpteenth time.

(Bless me Boys, for I have sinned. It has been one week since my last confession, I accuse myself of: lies, disobeyances, fights. Dashing through my apostle's creed to get to the car first. Only to find the engine idling, mother's dinner burning up; and the four angels singing Edelweiss by the windowseats. Only to be lurched into the *way back*, to share the miserly airspace with a beloved and flatulent black lab.

What did *you* get, one would ask.

One our father, two hail marys, came the ardent reply.

Me too, I said. The dog barking from his belfry, silent but deadly. And for these and all my sins, I am heartily sorry. Amen. So be it. For as far as I know there *is* no sin for wafting out the oeils-de-boeuf. For snaking up the Father O'Leary's black dress. To snap and sniff the holy garters or to squeeze two lumps.)

But I don't have all day standing here in the butt of the church, dreaming of my someday ordination. You can keep 'n' scratch your two prodigal sons. Vatican III. Access to god does not evolve with the rights of women and the emancipation of slaves! (faggot nigger-bitches; sticks and stones)

I *will* not wear the lacy doily; I *will* not wear the lacy doily. My eyes will not have their peripheries only. I will be commissioned instead: by a rare breed of apostles to gut and serve the saint's face to the snapdragons (subservient lawn statues in next life). I will plump and flour the loaves. I will love my mother. I will catch the big fish all alone out at sea while you go fishing on Sundays for some mirage. Some puddlefish. Some virgin.

Some abortion.

I will slap my father on the back, because he is like me. (Where is the end of your servitude? Haloed eyes? Black and blue? The children? Forced to watch?) Nothing is filthier than the subjugation of a mother.

Do not accept the cream-colored skin and the one jar of salve! (no virgin ever wrote no book)

I want to carry his coffin, I want to feel the weight of his body and bear the full pith of my dead on my shoulders.

He is my grandfather, sir. (Who is that crapulous and offensive monkey on yours?)

If Father is caught wearing the kilt he can always say, hey, I had paused only for a moment to put my bagpipes down. As for me, that last indiscrete moment I'll believe it all (hoping he is not around) or fail to comply:

? *can* a moody baby doom a yam ?

(The priest is frocked in fuscia velvets and I am bombed. He sprinkles us with an urn, 150 proof holy water, because we are your beloved.) The priest says cumulus omnibus and a great deal of dead Latin intervenes and the hokus pokus braggart in the frock, the royal taxidermist, stuffs you into your velvet clothes telling us your descension was psychosomatic (you murmur your own latin maledictions to the man who does not know your ass from adam).

Which is not to say, that the priest, a kind and portly man, did not bring a nun, one covered dish, and pickle and pimento loaf to the grieving home. He made the mortal mistake of telling her the beets had stained her mouth, and she could only smile a little crinkly confused smile, a rhubarb, and look away because she could not hear him (doesn't see too well) and I spun her around and shuffled her off patty-cake, patty-cake, toward a plate of deviled egg before the brute could have his way with her or swindle her savings.

And though I knew you liked white meat, puppa, and didn't like multicolored liver spots in your luncheon meats, I didn't let on. His behavior was inappropriate, he is not a bad man. (Although I would not touch *his* grandmother with the ten foot pole or dash her, in and out of the tongue of the flame, saying: Take this body. Eat this blood.)

Up on the altar in a decidedly phallic ritual the priest manufactures your absolution and I am willing to believe, not because it is plausible but because it is necessary. Just now.

Portrait of a Girl

The priest says you are delivered from your earthly state of imperfection. You would have said, "I beg your pardon." No, you would not. You went malignant. But that's how I like to remember you. Funny like that.

I listen as the cusps of your glottis open and close. Father, son, and holy ghost—sounds like another bachelor party, another gangbang another spring break at Lauderdale where yours truly jumps out of the cake (god's most intelligent creature after man), asking, did the ground hog see his shadow today?

I wedged into the confessional box like some Victorian tart squeezed into her whalebone corset. To the church I was only twelve but I was already the bicycle seat, the garter, the rose. These are not autotelic entities.

(God is there to remind you there is more than one way to go blind but we all know—that last act—is an act of Submission and I will not ruin you big day with what you already know.)

My father had a pair of thin Irish lips that blistered and pressed together like parchment. He always checked his emotions. He put the obdurate silence in the family tree; he was on the mantel, our family crest, the mastadon; a gravely concerned man, a king. He had a very matter-of-fact and made-up mind. With the stoicism with which he faced death every day he could not stomach the peas.

His heart squished out all over his sleeves.

He was the man poised in front of the coatroom, handing over the family coats, posturing to the maitre d'. (The kids will have the shirley temples whiskey sour for the wife I'll have my vodka martini straight up.)

He was kind to his mother; I think he noticed the one tarnished clip-on onyx earring.

I imagined him swirling with us kids in teacups in Storybookland but in real life, he was not always himself, he was his animadversion.

He worked too hard.

Twice a year, in some hypothetical world, he became the fisherman he was, fly-fishing in his Eddie Baeur boots, swatting back the black flies; on Sundays he spread bags of peat moss and loam; the bag said *compressed sphagnum*, and I knew that, like the words still coming off the dictation long after he had fallen asleep, *Gestational Trophoblastic Neoplasm*, I would remember them.

He brought home new flies, a mallard doormat or a duck sculpture and this was as much sloth or pleasure he allowed himself and it was enough.

I loved him most when he showed up at the breakfast table with a patch on his face, or that moment when he came home; the severe moment when he softened, removed his necktie; that moment when he squeak-cleaned the spaces between his teeth and clucked his gums. (When mother said there's a scenic overlook up ahead; handing out quarters he jammed his brakes and said *wait until I stop the car*—the five of us clamoring to the two telescopes and the dog again in the front seat; steering like a tank our two eyes to Old Man of the Mountain or some otherwise ignobled overhang.)

When he poked his head into our room and said *no monkey business.*

He could be ruthless picking eggshells out of his omelet, boning his fish, complaining that the spaghetti was soggy; something always alive missing overdone. He would yell out THERE ARE NO ICE CUBES THE FEEDER IS EMPTY WHAT'S THAT SMELL, telling my mother that she ought

to keep more raspberry jam in the house and every time
mother cooked a pot of corned beef and cabbage he asked
DID THE DOG PISS ON THE RUG

We send our playboys to the Senate we both agree,
while the artist suffers inimically in the one room for what
little she knows.

We both have the short fuse but only I burn at both ends.

He has a wife who cooks his vegetables.

I was always glad to see the chickadees at the bird
feeder; the mourning doves made him angry and a pervad-
ing sense of injustice would ruin my whole morning, as if
mother had overcooked the peas. Again.

The time the topsoil washed away with it the front lawn
he said Judas Priest and called Chemlawn himself.

When he burned effigies of himself out on the front lawn
I wished he wouldn't.

During vacations he was already up each morning for
his five a.m. dip into the frozen Atlantic.

His lip trembled and the pallor of his constricted face
tells me I have appropriated from him more than a sense of
the quintessential facts and that he loves his father.

Because of him I am one of the hibakusha (explosion-
affected people). Which is to say, I do not always spoon out
the after-dinner mints, take all things to the maxima and
minima; spent my youth in frantic emulation, glad to find
out I had his astigmatism, too, and always knowing where
he could find the nozzle of the hose. He is however, a man
not to be contradicted (and you know how relentless and
good I am at that). I appropriate the insides of parentheses
and he balks at the ERA (I was never up with the birds I
never knew what all the early risers knew instinctively by
dawn; father, I was never you; the son who hadn't a pot to
piss in). But it is a thankless story, all; for I know it is his

pot I piss in and I could not apologize enough for all of my advantages.

(It was Nietzche, daddy, who held us in a half-nelson, all our lives. It is he who tampered with the weather. He who set out after us with the closely following cloud. (tiptoeing and disappearing when we looked back)

Sent by you to the red room, gutting my first poem, I have contemplated the enormity of my life, my first book of feelings. Regenerating our hands, hearts and feet, we have beckoned and fought our tragic and deeply-felt lives with a terrible, loving will.

When he pared down an apple he ate it seeds and all.

He was no hypocrite.

He was honest and intense and his face was strangely prickly, like a strawberry.

There were perhaps some discrepancies and infidelities in the parable of father and son.

You could not forgive yourself for something, puppa. The son who pointed up up and away to the aurora borealis and left home having already made his own way; the prodigal son whose monolithic pride one-upped your hard-earned lackadaisical life in Maine, your tinkering your vaudeville one-liners; the son you boosted up into the highfalutin world using two crummy hands as rungs, your own slipshod and ordinary failures his stepping stones to next life. He had nothing you could not find in the obscurity of your own pockets and I tell you he is happiest with what little you taught him spreading loam.

(For him you were the man of venison and moose, up for the five a.m. duckhunt; for him you went out into the frozen five a.m. morning to start the car and scrape the windshield

89

and because he liked birches best you always said the birches are looking good, son, and you seemed to have an extra kick the days the birds took to the feeder for thistle and sunflower and you'd run out and swat the squirrels from the feeder, gad outta there, not because you were mad at the wildlife or because she'd told you Winthrop! he is on his way home but because you were like me a small child earning his love) By jesus I've inherited that chirping boy scout's honor too, but I could cross that line back into Vacationland and spend a day in bed. Resolute as a prussian ox, he pulled his own weight. You were both men from the no hunting no trespassing generation of the state-a-maine and your dirt roads were sometimes long impassible private drives.

I think you spoke a silent, surrogate language, too.

Along the back roads of Maine, every twenty miles, a dairy shack; just far enough.

When he went out to mow the lawn or tie one on I popped my head into his room and couldn't be happier.

Tonight you order your meatloaf well-done puppa at the Chuckwagon restaurant in Rumford Maine, tell your proud and prodigal son and all the gallants at the mill, "Madame Bovary, c'est moi." Everyone claims to have lived on your block. Everyone! (She saw it first, in your penmanship, it had a kind of artistic flair unbecoming a workman's hands, and she knew you, way back when.)

Your wife turns to you and says, "L'Oétat, c'est moi?"

Yes, I march against the liquidation of your hen-pecked milltowns, the eradication of your window boxes, stuck in their ways; in my recurrent fantasy, and full of face, the Mr. and Mrs. T. order the meatloaf; I keep you in snuffboxes, now, cantankerous little people who I can take out and love.

In my recurrent fantasy, because I loved you, I am not afraid to grow old.

No one ever really knew the man of venison and moose, his twin sisters Alfreda and Almeda, of whom he never spoke.

And then we heard it, the polite poof!

Close Your Eyes and Think of Dublin

"and nobody knew so well
how to frighten Miss Clavel."

As long as we are together and the silence is compulsory, it happens; we bellow forth, two heathens.

No matter how many times we laughed, it was always at the man who looked like his dog. We laughed at communion, the conference of degrees, or a big bazoom; anybody sacred or smarty-pants or snooty; the crippled and the laid in state; anyone by the name of madame or mister we imagined without a stitch on; we laughed at persons of principle or pedigree; pacons, pomeranians or pekingese would do it. We'd break down staring into a mash of avocado and sprouts. When together we were bound to run into some dimwit nutcracker postal clerk confounding himself counting out stamps, or a woman in boas and furs, speaking all in wide vowels, or a child with a great impedimediment or the staid presence of the head of the household, grouchy at the end of his long hard day; she would bury her face in her napkin, or shuffle away to the sink to quiet herself, always that moist ruddiness of her cheeks, that fullness of face, that flabbiness of her neck; her gassing, spewing good time, as she tried to collect herself in front of her son; tears welling and sputtering; we went into stitches, the both of us; we'd better stop our foolishness she'd say or *honestly*, at *my* age, but like the peach cobbler, the brown betty, the three bean salad, we went the way of all flesh; and we were apt to laugh, to go on laughing, long after we were told to stop.

It was always those hiked-up ramparts of Chastity and Serendipity that did it. The nun who had taught me catechism since grade one, who had snapped her fingers and hushed us all to hell in a husky whisper in the unrelenting acoustics of church. Her slow and heavy gestation as she dragged her bulky body swayback from the room, and the few greasy untucked strands of hair outside the headpiece, convinced me that she lacked self-knowledge, and perhaps, needed a bath.

With all her busywork, punctuality and order, she had seemed curiously dispassionate, and there was a good chance that she would appear there that day. She frightened me because she didn't scold you she just gave you the sanctified morbid look and turned away.

That body was no temple and I wondered, what was it, exactly; a crew cut, almost—asexual, but for the few greasy strands; they had men's names (Sister Michael Marie); feigning helplessness they were disciplinarians with no opinions and missionaries in Africa, having their mail censored by the Vatican, I couldn't figure it; perhaps she kept a pet rodent in her cell, yes, it was one of those new postulants who kept her in the kneeling posture without moving for so long. I might have chiseled to China by now or had a paring knife baked into the meringue pie but I suppose she liked it, I suppose it was a little like Rush, selling them to this Order or another, getting new girls. Instead of fraternity parties they had a Particular Friend. Yes, once from the front pew I smelled her breath and I imagined two nuns holding hands; she had eaten something strange for breakfast like poached egg and cold biscuits and yes, there was a moist crumb of goat cheese on her upper lip and I knew it all along.

That's what happens when you censor yourself at the subconscious level. The meat goes bad. The breath starts to smell, a kind of dominance. You must first carve your breakfast into quarters before you eat it. She ate gonads for breakfast, two marbled eggs, with her small lapdog, a Lhasa apso from Tibet, their hair over their eyes, into the food. And a fat cat named Romeo, too. Not a woman but a marsupial, fumbling for her bible and beads, reaching deep into a large front pocket for her wristwatch before she set us free; the incrustation of her male habit built like tartar on her teeth and she was cruel to children.

I knew there was some hidden ecstasy felt kneeling in the silence of the one next to you, for I had known, sat circumspectly and perfectly still, through the three hours of Stations of the Cross, only touching the enslaved leg of the one next to me, and I could easily imagine the whole catechism class, there on its knees, thrilled to its senses, unable to concentrate on god at all, but attaching, instead, to the indefatigable windbags of her nun's face, disappearing with words that came and went imperceptibly in a garble off her lips, flubbering like the jowls of a St. Bernard, out through the opened windows, drifting off into the lost sputter of the bewitched voices playing outside, wafting up the nun's habit, goaded by guilt and fear, while her waxing strictures moved in and behind her yellowed teeth like an old decrepit fray of dental floss, and we agitated with impure thoughts and impure manipulations, crimes committed in the sacristy, in the alleged and thinking stages; the fantasizing of what it was like to pass each other in the hall in total silence, to be so constricted from the out-of-doors; and above and beyond we all wondered the one thing: what it was like to plant the kiss on the forehead of one so holy.

She had spotted me once, with the pinch of her fingers, when I had fallen back into the front pew, fainting and swooning under the spotted and changing lights, and come

up gnashing, blinking through the mottle of my eyes, up at
her, and she had told me in her phobic hyper-correct speech
and her faintly rotting breath to put my head down between
my knees, that god would look after me; but still brimming
with the waspy terror of having been woken by some bad-
breathed stranger from a moist sleep, I had asked, instead,
for my mother.

Although it seemed a poignant curiosity to me that,
where she had resumed a kind of tingling circulation in my
head, she had cut it off again in my arm, it was somehow
vaguely comforting that she herself had punctured me and
issued these instructions for my well-being, and that I
would be there again at 4:30 on Thursday afternoon; and
that, on this particular morning, years later, I had returned
with my Compulsories to rise a final time, to speak in
unison five times, "Good afternoon Sister Michael Marie!
Good Afternoon!" (though I had appended my catechism
and had her fullblown out to sea, drawn and quartered in
ways not permissible to think).

Washing up on the beaches of Lilliput she is blindfolded
and made to play kissing cousins with the whole town. The
children get there first, tying her to the sand with the
cincture of her habit and driving quick painless little stakes
into the rigid gimp of her hands, flagellating her nosehairs
softly with the tassel ends.

Soon there are little fallen men everywhere shaking
and jiggling into the quagmire of her belly, counting the
bands of her deposed midsection like the coils of a soft
decaying tree; lines form in the welts of higher elevations
where the elastic waistband of her partially unfurled underpants has tracked her flesh; and sliding down the yellow

creases where her fat changed directions, she began to quiver and shake as they, in their near-fatal landslides, their laughter in remission, climb back up, bouncing, rolling over and over into the fluffy folds of her moonwalk.

Others, lifting the bangs of her pixie and the frontispiece of her artifact, look in, peering under panels and the starched guimpe and from within pockets; shimmying like firemen down the one greased strand into the meringue; uncovering moles, snapping and unsnapping her contraptions, experimenting with the blowsy contortions of her face, folding and unfolding her hands, covering and uncovering her eyes, doing and undoing the sign of the cross, performing mortifications, taking custody of the senses and the snags and hitches of her giant brassiere, skipping along spider veins and playing in the dark ombre patchwork under her eyes; a set of triplets traces the Stigmata, tickling the arch of her hands, feet, and sides while she groans and tries to get away.

One enterprising young boy boxes against the perturbation by dodging in and out of the battering rise and fall of her adam's apple. Another boy goes gootchie goo straight for the rib and the lad doing a headstand on the tip of her nose has fallen off, coming at him, while a patient little girl in a pink tutu does a pirouette in his place.

Soon there are pulleys and swings yanking on her prosthetic devices, trespasses at her feet, scaffolding everywhere; cams and rods and cylinders rocking, pummelling, hammering, with calibrated, discriminating strokes and unremitting pistons—and out of nowhere comes a blur of sirens, a megaphone, the skirmish of polished boots taking over; the incumbent and the chief of police yelling out: no whittled ends to insert! no honed edges! no slow moving rotor saws! And as the public stenographer taps out the whole morse code on her slab of municipal bedrock from the

Portrait of a Girl

back of the paddywagon, she yells, too: no running no roughnecking! law and order! please!

They look up for a millisecond or less (who knows what time could mean to them) but they keep feeding her tiny sweet sacraments and a bubbly Eucharistic house wine. One reassures her that he is only undoing her corset to tie her to the bleachers. She is propped up brilliantly, the town fathers agree, accessible from the front and rear, with small ramps for the handicapped.

Everywhere they came and went AWOL agog beserk amok splat. The whole teeming town pushing and shoving to the rig; oh, there were a few who stood by clutching their purses and children, or opening their windows in small increments only to shake their mops, but they were in the minority.

She tried to hold her breath until she duly expired but she ended up letting out one big animal grunt which pleased them entirely on the moonwalk.

Woof! Woof!

I'll say.

Get her on a rollaway!

Immobilize the neck!

Pulse and Respiration!

Nurse!

Dead one says, dead for ten days.

Check the tag! Is she registered?

Measuring the wingspan, one postulated that it had been devised to fly early on in its evolution.

Size 12 1/2 feet the cobbler blatted out!

Don't go in, a jewish mother says to her only son, you'll probably have to marry it.

Don't let her swallow her tongue! said the son.

Politicians came and went, making their arbitrary and assinine speeches, passing out fliers of their families.

What is it one said.
What it is! said another jacking up to look.
She be a *bad* mother—
Um um.
Slap me five.
Out of my way said one, bespectacled professor emeritus of the humanities, grabbing the field glasses from an ornithologist calling out to the rare bird, chip chip chiparee.
Reeeeeee.
It's dextrorotary said one, adjusting his microscope; it's your spitting image said his wife.
She is carrion one said (uniformly black) professor of black history.
A look or a touch! A cop or a feel! 25 cents.
Pardon me? said another.
Don't touch it said a mother.
It should be turned like a fatty shish kebab twice a day, said a Ph.D., poking at it like some beached white Leviathan.
Face is pale raise the tail!
Large-pored and flatulent!
Grandiloquence and largesse!
It doesn't shave its legs.
Ugh.
"That sea beast
Leviathan, which God of all his works
Created hugest that swim the ocean stream."
Paradise Lost! quoth another.
Queensize pantyhose.
(A whale by any other name.)
Amphibia!
Sir Prufrock!
Sent by the French!
Check the underarms.

Portrait of a Girl

Noblesse Oblige.
I can tell by the rrr' s.
She's full of it said one.
I am sure of it, said another.
One was convinced, him having said so.
Wait 'til the press gets here, we'll know for sure.
A celestial body dropped like a formless lump from the
Vatican ceilings cried another, nibbling on the cheesy taste
of her doughy thighs and buttocks.
36 Flavors! yelled the confectioner, handing out small
pink taster spoons.
Its mother will never again touch it.
(I wouldn't, said another) barely venturing outside her
parenthesis to speak the awful Truth. Let go of my arm,
said her husband.
She's here one said.
She's not said the other.
Ship's Ahoy! Cried some from her stomach, where they
were patting and rolling out the already patented dough.
One heard the rancid rumblings of the stomach acids
and ran.
One having seen him running ran too.
Praise the Lord! cried one.
(It's a *girl* spoke another.)
One even tries to do away with himself, so sure he is it's
the end of the world. He comes at her from the rear with a
periscope and an aerosol can. I've found it, he cries, peering
over the starburst rim into the revolving splices of rank
browns (a kaleidoscope of horrors as she wiggles and
worms). Her eyes percolate, she tries to sit Erect (the grace
of god the only currency she knows) she squeezes as she
tries to dislodge him kindly and he falls in and sputtering
out again is sent like a blubbering balloon ballyhooing across

the land in a discrete gust of typhonic air in and out of the embattered throngs.

Aye! It's only the criminal element that's passed, says one at her window, shaking her mop, the clutch and jerk of her elbows sure of his divine culpability and scratching her ear to get to her nose.

An etymologist tries to match her up with his insect collection and has a smear of something on his cheesecloth.

Others scrape it onto their plates or into a petri dish, swashing their tongues around surreptitiously for what they already know.

Some are cloistered around, listening for Providence to strike again, or a Great Flood.

Others in rank and file move on; still others, mill around. She is losing patience fast. (I imagined their swarming little bodies felt like pushpins, armies of them, or feathers.) Why, with misplaced pogo sticks bounding out of nowhere, lurid botanists, disenchanted mudwrestlers, father-son outings, rodeos, luau, mardis gras, clambakes, oyster-shucking festivals, symposiums, food fights, medical conventions, somniferous artists, jewish mothers and rhythm and blues; what with kissing booths, pinball machines, Donkey Kong, a hanging and a tar and feathering a little later on; what with Arabs drubbing and rooting for oil in follicles and areoles, and driving on the wrong side of the street, what with all the false starts wild goose chases trap doors; somebody's bound to tumble down the laundry chute or lose his mother.

For some it is just another day at the beach.

A matriarch rubs and blubbers over to what looks like a picnic table, flags it with the cone of her lumbering umbrella, and scratches out her sandpiper commands, doing those long yawning calisthenics with her jowls; then stretching out her picnic lunch and two dozen children in oversized flip-flops over the bayou flats; then sinking into her chaise lounger, hubba bubba buddha, with the great Pprrpffrrppfff.

On the contrary, some have embarked on their solitary and singular vocations. One is pulling quarks and particles of lint and all kinds of hypothetical snuff out of her inflamed bellybutton; one has called it fairy dust and one says it's carbon 14; one with the butt of her broom says it's ground dirt. A disgruntled geologist grabs the radioactive isotope and sells it, per mole of solute, to teenagers looking for a new inhalant. An explorer has marked it *equator* and is meandering south to claim the rest; a mathematician is heading north and east to intersect the two legs of the triangle and a fife and drum corps will be there to greet them both.

A whole family heads down 95 South from their vacationland in Maine, passing a strolling minstrel with some castanets and a blind girl looking for her dyslexic brother. The dog hangs his head outside the window, drooling, knowing what will happen once they get there. A geriatric member of the explorer's club has carried his kayak over the shoulder for many years and will unload it on the first whitewater he sees.

A bag lady whistling through her teeth zigzags up the Atlantic coastline looking for King Crab, picking the juices from the legs and succulents washing up, clucking her teeth, Cluck, Cluck, before moving on.

A zealous scout leader, a gentleman and a virgin, takes the boy scouts on their first overnight outing and there are plenty of brownies and bluebirds begging to go along; soon the troops are singing Kumbaya! Kumbaya! My Lord! and, moving right along, marshmallows drawn, look for a campfire and something to spook them in the night.

A frat boy, hanging from the night before, goes out to find and jumpstart his car. A craggy face comes down off the mountain for the first time, looking for his dog. A girl walking around seeing all the possibilities, could not make up her mind.

A psychic lights the night with a candle, perches, chanting, on a nipple while the Kenya club of Manhattan prepares to film a documentary on the tiny flora and fauna of the pulsing African bush. Crouched off in the distance an indian rubs two hands together.

A gentleman caller waits serenely under the mistletoe.

A small boy curls up in her nose and she twitches but does not sneeze.

More and more children are unaccounted for; there are fewer on tippytoes or peering in, and the homesick Visad has lost his India, has gone brooding over the unknown topography, for the one mole.

A bunch of poets and knowing types say very little, and gallop away like gazelles, from one clearing to the next. (Art, the wet spots in their eyes?)

A clingy girl tries to put her hair up in rollers while another presses her face ardently into Sister's front pouch and begs to be told a story. One hangs upside down like a koala bear asking does she have children of her own. Others just as needy fuse like barnacles to her mossy face or put posies gingerly in her pockets; one hauls a fledgling ashplant out from the verdant hillside onto her chest and stands there suffering from dependence, passivity, and no self-esteem.

The story goes on and on.

She lies there, leavening slowly, smelling sour or of yeast; children in plaid skirts and blazers are sent skipping rope out onto her chest and she is made to recite the silences in a maladroit, singsong way: ordinary, small, or simple;

103

solemn, sacred, or profound. She is confused and angry as some young boys are sent hacking and whistling into her hairy underarms.

They have finished looting her pockets and a mass of men are staring into some wet membrany things rolled up in tissues. Each time they pass it along she issues a kind of reproach.

With a giant shoehorn a bunch of indeterminate old women with many children and things to do have yanked off her big fuzzy hushpuppies, and a few have absconded with her orthopedic stockings, blasting her olfactory living and battling for squatter's rights to the linings, while another lady in a lamé gown paints appliqués on her toes and gives off catlike electrical charges.

A clique of teenage girls beebuzz and pluck at her toe hairs.

She'll have lovely well-disciplined toes said one, unanimously.

Marvelous, they agree.

Clipped to the cuticle and sanded back with the stiffest of emery, they said, 10 gidgets filing away.

And soon it was the place to be for sunning, jamming, and grooming.

Their mentor, chiselling away at the hangnail, speaks of redoing the neck panel in lavender.

She'll have the only feet immaculate enough to kiss says one.

Had they not been so modest, embarks another. Perched like an ibis on the small toe.

Fun to ravage though says one male onlooker.

A row of ten exemplary virgins, all lily-white and ready to go, says another.

Never having been exposed by so much as a Roman sandal or a simple V gleamed another.

Just think.

A thong between the toes, even.

A perfect ten.

He started to frisk the spaces between her toes and this led to a ransacking assault by the others.

The felines let out the usual cacophony and skipped off to tell the others. Some returned home to talk on the phone and the rest stayed on to watch, superfluous and smiling.

Snitches! he cried but he kept on, the leader of them all, slapping the slab of driftwood against the waiting palate of his hand in the rhythm of the impending encroachment while more girls looked dreamily on.

(She is jittery and pale and religious, she lurches but can not sit up from the nailed-shut coffin of her belief.)

One swaggers over to the big toe and nibbles it from the side. The others chide in, baby, baby, too hot for *hell*, nudging her curried digits with their ballistic noses and she tingles where another plunks his elbows down to eat (she cannot help but think of her P.F. can she now) and soon the calamity at her feet has wafted up; they have called each other numbskull and clobbered each other in turn.

There are other assignations, tickle and tweak, peek-a-boo and piggly wiggly, back at the head; they are already chipping small souvenirs off the plaque of her teeth; one is carving her Initials into a secret place and one is taking what seems like forever to tow away the rear molar, in a wheelbarrow. One has rolled, with the help of the others, a pumice stone to the elbow. There are messengers passing holy cards announcing her long-awaited arrival—a curious mixture of child, eunuch and man.

Step right up.

Get yer foot-long hot dogs mile-high hamburgers.

The fun! The flying! The fantastic!

See the indescribable the invincible the insurmountable all-poodle revue!

See the irrefragable the irrefrangible the inerrable the ineffable the INDESCRIBABLE UNMENTIONABLE!

The testing, testing, and then the tap, tap, can you hear me, sends audio-erotic whispers through her crackly spine. He will shoot himself out every half hour saying (*look at meee a humancannonball*)!

By now they have named her Brother Helga; news has swept through the impoverished town.

We've caught ourselves a Carmelite!

We've caught ourselves a Man!

It's the St. Louis of France, stupid!

Is not!

Is!

Not!

One says Benedictine, one says no.

One swears it's the Immaculate Heart of Mary jellywashed on the beach.

One says brown and black, that's all I know; one says Bride of Christ! and one says Over my dead body! She's mine!

Soon the feet are inhabited by those of race, sex, creed, and color. Orphans, alcoholics, homosexuals, neurotics, writers, crippleds, coloreds, junkies, jews, mothers, ax murderers, nihilists—you know the rest—all having arrived, bleary-eyed and drunk, from the Archetype at the head, washing into the flowing cloaca of human awareness and then—toe wedge.

It seems so inevitable now; they have blueprints for everything, they have almanacs, kites, keys, lanterns, candelabra, bifocals, lightening bugs, search warrants, german shepards, walkmen, toothpicks, grappling irons, a coat hanger, badges, spermicide, secret service, remote and mission control, microprocessors magpies popguns, sensors, feelers, mimes, sheet music, art, Alanon and a holiday inn; they are armed with pointers, pincers, and photons, a helix and a harpoon, a single magnifying glass and armies of panhandlers and priests; there are cartographers, watchmakers, astronomers, backtrackers, beekeepers, topographical maps, trustees, a syndicated columnist and one even knows the weather.

A small black boy the size of a gnat has engineered a giant cuff for her rising barometric pressure and before his mother catches him he samples a bit of paté between the adjacent feets, spitting her out, complaining that his food is not pure enough.

Cornered by the glare of two souped-up headlight stares, the few remaining bobtail deer are caught rubbing wet animal noses (the rumors of cock and cunt pump through conscientious suburbs) and they gleam back the sad flourescent night eyes of animal penetration, to give them time to look back and understand—why everything else is invisible—suspending flight for a moment before they are driven down to the fag leather cities which is no place for gentle animals (leaving the delicate paw prints that mean nothing to them).

She thickens, grows swollen and starchy, and is forced to redefine the lines and ligature of her newly partitioned body; she will grow lithe and wise as a panther or she will live bottled up inside, moored to the couch and TV.

One has stationed himself by the lower quadrant with a seismograph; the search expands into the microanatomy, gets so small the leathery eye of the fruitfly can now be fathomed along with astrophysics and the extraterrestrial moving eyes on rotor-stalks; scavenging lakes no bigger than the size of a capsule, the animal rescue league has impounded a truckload of small household pests from what looks like low tide.

Yuppies are arriving at the shipwreck at her feet, walking dogs in henna, saffron, taupe, or mauve.

One surveying the crumbling landscape pulls a rope saying a bit my way, accentuate the arch. But his accomplice is the first to announce he is no good at following directions and hollers the forecast down to the feet.

Some say it was the Chinese who started it, playing ping pong to escape the dry cleaning business. Others blame the visiting dignitaries, Eritrean cabbies, and messenger boys riding in and out of and against oncoming traffic, expatriates at the feet.

One militant black woman says I told that child to stay out of the moors!

Streams trickle where Carter had marked her flesh.

A bunch of small fry have found a spout.

One girl has something stuck in her braces.

Pagans are anointing themselves with a queer metallic wine.

Little girls are more subservient than ever, have found other vestiges, mossy, overgrown.

Barnacles have moved to other fuzzy wuzzy places.

Two sprockets are up and the psychic gone.

One thinks it is a fire hydrant and has lifted a hind leg.

One opinionated man assures the rest it is an underground sprinkler system (he is a civil engineer).

Children begin to come oozing down off the waterslides; hobgoblins with puny projectiles prepare to relieve themselves in the bushes, and a dairy farmer, circumnavigating his face, subsidizes his dreams and is happy for a moment because the crops will grow this year.

A motorcade heads for an erogenous zone to commemorate the farmer; the president is in it, fitted with a bulletproof vest and an asbestos suit, but he has forgotten his seat cushion.

Perhaps the natives are having a block party, one remarks, leagues away, noticing the rising urban humidity.

Along come two child sleuths and a prodigal dog, holding the map with the big red X. Their mother does not care about them.

A jewish mother hands her son a safety net but he ignores the growing osmolarity.

A little retarded girl with poor proprioception has been given a popsicle.

One plays pachisi and is now throwing his last man Home.

One calls for the Department of Public Works to mop the humidity off her face, but it is too late.

Some little charge has dragged his little brother into a dank tunnel to see Oz and another child dumber yet thinks her inner ear the boardwalk of Candyland.

She begins to heave but the elder child has already run back out (covered with the Protean limesalts, calling for his mother).

Don't go in! It's got a giant growing *thing*—

A cat stretches itself.

The truncated ear of the dog.

A town yawns.

The old man has a moment of lucidity and yelps.

Suddenly it is happening, little Austrians in khaki climbing shorts excavating in the alps, two others running first for two flags, droves of schoolchildren playing marco polo, forming a human train into the woods and the clankety clank of rusting human axles puffing and wheezing as a train comes out of nowhere and little handmaids of christ rapelling up the pubic bone (a quick prayer for continence) leads two boys to start a brushfire in her eyebrows a couple of wayward chaps basking in the steamheat of the underground vents too hot for hell thar she blows curds and way yodelling down for the others to come on up while she sings in a complete crisis of faith *Salve Salve* (send the altar girls) but they are already running barrels over the knob of her rosary beads each one as scrupulous as the next; and two screaming redheads riding the Flume send back little electroshocks to the left and to the right, waving to family and friends, so many prayers, so many transgressions, venial and mortal, out the window, all at once, one after another (as the tachometer resets to zero) (a frantic switchboard operator plugging in dials 0) calling for more horseradish, a few more little medallions of beef, an ice cube, to move this way or that, to the front or back, or out of the way.

And then came Stevie's bright red truck screeching fullspeed up the middle.

I wish you could see her face.

Hands folded tightly under the holy scapular, she reports to Chapter of Faults Monday morning to meet her confessor in that slow measured pace, mumbling of a remote island, just a speck to the slowly marooned, a day of feast, of Gregorian Chant, gifts of the Holy Spirit, the Key to the Town; yes and in the throes of an immaculate conception, if telling the truth sets her free, she can tell Father, "I broke Silence five times."

I imagined that she had a sparse graying little tuft of hair down there and the idea repelled me. She always incited in me the desire to see her as her opposite—writhing or sliding hush hush onto a whoopee cushion or into a seat reserved for the family.

The sanctified naiveté of the order around me told me it was a church run not by god, but by men, by the funny little men who lived inside, and that they could not be blamed, really, for what they could not know or imagine. I untied her, knowing someday I would have to find my own words, tell it to the beekeeper, my own father, the groundskeeper, the Lurch in the monkeysuit, full of self-contempt and revolted by human self-disclosure.

No, I was no ordinary parishioner, and she lay before me not vast and white, but like a crippled insect plied to the sand, with no strictly contemplative life of her own—just a lot of auxillary and self-flagellating legs bestowed with a certain singular horrible vocation.

I knew I would have to rise up from centuries old pushpins and move—those ancillary and abdicating legs—to a religious calling of my own, worse than poverty, obedience, and chastity, because I knew and I confessed to myself that I could rightfully eat meat every day of the week (try as I did to fall useless and prostrate before Him on Fridays), and that trying to work his face into the panels and walls was no proper way to thank him, and no way to love anybody, much less god.

By jesus I'd fall before him prostrate calling for grace if I saw his wife staring off into the distance at Lourdes, too.

(I am still attired in purple, never having finished Lent, or having given up successfully the one thing I loved most I could not go to that mountain and kill my mother if she knew I was killing her and not know why.)

But as the Canon Law does not entitle its pledges to their formal goodbyes, to greet the dying at home, or at the very least to keep a particular friend, I'll have to go ahead and write to Rome, calling for my dispensation soon.

God knows I loved my grandfather more than that.

Portrait of a Girl

I must keep the premonitory urge to laugh because
when she shook, the whole city of Lilliput came down.
Five times in silence.
Her whole life.
God knows I speaketh the Truth more often in a day.

And when the latent mother superior appeared that
day, dragging the gangplank leg, leading with the black
wedge shoe, heading straight for our front row pew, the
silence built, and I imagined Winthrop taking aim against
the wide sprawling ecstacy (some sad and horrible provoca-
tion), and stoking up her skirt, egging us on, watching her
bray, slide the hoof, swishing around, ninny ninny neigh,
ninny ninny neigh; I looked at him and then at her and she
hit us with the leg the woodplank pew; the snag in my
throat, a large bolus, I yelped, I caught myself in time, then
I started hiccupping and couldn't stop. The juices flowed
back up the nun's leg to coagulate and defile. Wives turned
to turnip and cattle. She had some disgusting miscellany
in her purse. Hoping not to laugh, avoiding anywhere a
bosom might rise and heave, the eye of some aspirating
organ; she moved in: bent over to kick up the kneeler; he
hung that WIDE LOAD sign on the beamend arse of mother
superior and Winthrop she was saying you ol' dope now lie
down and tend to your affairs but Winthrop like a pirate
bandit dog quipped out of the one eye BROADER THAN
THE BROADSIDE OF A BARNDOOR and that's when we
heard it, we three, the living and the dead, the polite poof!
    Nana thought and there but for the grace of god go I, and
all hell broke loose on our one impetuous face. (Yes, puppa,
we buried you with the clicking teeth, the laughing bag, the
fake puke.)

It was you sitting up to give us all a good scare.

You bet your sweet ass.

We the tittering sisters of mercy spill back into our clothes and I think how we together live for these tender moments when teacher turns her back.

(We couldn't help it and we both know we are not the only catalysts in the church. Nobody can believe we have taken our foolishness this far and we both know we are incorrigible, too.)

We are summoned to our places. Some Oracle wants a word with us. We shuffle two abreast. I nudge her. She nudges me. We brace ourselves; together we titter in the blank white light between words that are spoken and words that are not, raw as nerve. The curtain opens or closes. We have performed acts of consequence and repercussion, violated the three simulated points of the triangle, offended Father, son, and holy ghost. We do or do not get the look of indignation.

Ma, he said, You want a peppermint?

Don't be cross with me, she said. And then she was crying.

Something told me that somewhere somebody was thinking that I had made her cry. (I couldn't help it. It was one of those plaster vixens come to me and said, "Maybelle, kindly engage the mourners in a game of charades." But they were already enjoying their game of simon says came the reply, but it's no use arguing.)

For my penance I might only have to fix my grandmother a cold drink. Bam Bam or Pebbles? Barney or Fred? Wilma or Betty? What'll it be? (bottom of your glass)

(don't be so goddamned beastly funny your grandfather's dead and your grandmother needs a drink)

What will it be ma grand-mère—le chocolat or peppermint?

Portrait of a Girl

She'd be there at my bed anyway with a fistful of cookies
and a jar of salve.

Much later she would say *Honestly* if it's not one thing
it's another.

She tripped over the May Tag repairman and broke her
collarbone trying to get to the potato chips. They told her
she was lucky it wasn't her hip and I suppose she felt the
way he did when they told him he looked well.

There were kleenexes everywhere. An irate mother-in-
law kept fishing quarks out of her wash and I said it was me.
But she knew. Mothers always know.

She pressed her face into the pane waiting for Christmas and told the company *I don't see too well.* Oh, she says,
along in years, getting on; and there are chunks of greased
snow heaving here and there, in alleys, and behind cars.
They drop off fenders and melt back into the streets.

On Christmas eve she Bing and I danced the polka on
the living room rug; she danced somewhere she had danced
before under the on-again-off-again living room lights.

In defiance over dishes she and I (we three) got the old
holiday rag, she in her rumpled housecoat and me in
mother's lampoon apron, we did dishes the one-step two-
step and I swatted and slopped the dirty dishrag into her
bazooms or beamend behind and she said *shoosh shoosh*
and while I swilled the leftover half-carafes with the red
rolling waves of crepe paper I said *tora tora* and she ducked
and came at me calling me lady or lady jane then she well
what was it exactly so beastly funny in there in the kitchen,
you two (some dimwit nutcracker postal clerk confounding
himself) fa la la fa la la and before she ran into the bathroom
I picked the piece of decomposing crepe paper off her lip

leaving a raspberry green stain where it had melted into her cheek and she rinsed her underpants in infamy while I picked up the fallen hairwebs and the balled-up kleenexes as they dropped from the flabby sleeves of her housecoat and her camouflage fart spray smelled like yesterday's azaleas.

I caught her pouring over her Christmas cards with her gluey oversized bug glass and she made me read aloud each line of the Hallmark card or rather I read them to her because I loved her. Violet and blue and I love you. Again she said. Read me that poem. She kept writing more cards her brain blinking on and off it was Christmas eve forgetting to cross her t's we sent out doubles and triples to be sure and we spoke of her departed husband an elegant penman who made a life of signing her cards.

I helped her with her shower, old woman, my nana, how I loved her lukewarm, without a stitch on, putting her hands down there in a V where she pinched and wizened off, her crumbling fanny her breast pink as a thrush and when in an exquisite aside she turned to me and said please don't let them put me in a nursing home I said no, never. (roses and violets)

The windshield of a Subaru.

Hold my thumb that's what the oldtimers used to say when they were about to fart, she told me, climbing into the shower, forgetting to cover her crotch (those must be the dugs, I thought, the shrunken paps) and you little lady will not be pinned by the nurse who says and how is Mrs. T this morning, you will not be scolded for wandering off, you are my own nana. (you deviled egg you, patting at the inkstain of your cattycorner face you)

So often I showed my reverence by serving the florid sentimental spaces on Hallmark cards and before bed we read each one, once more, aloud.

She left the door cracked so I would peep in to say hey, you with the beamend, did you take your Metamucil? Muffy, I call her, tonight, muffy, muffins, dumplings (she bubbles and gases) because she has lilac babybreath and because her skull is still soft.

And sometimes late at night I would hear her voice coming down from the upstairs and she said Mae Mae have you got a chocolate bar Mae what time is it what are we doing up. Then I would hear her climbing out of bed, a sort of thump, thump, and then the munch of her bedslippers the nebeneinander and the soft crunch of the floor as she shuffled past the nightlight rebounding off the walls muttering to herself *they'll think I'm soused* weaving into the bathroom, *there, there*, plunking herself down.

Downstairs on Christmas morning I found her on the couch rattling the old wrappers again the wrappers of her Holiday Sampler, crunching fistfuls of colored popcorn against her face; she stared straight ahead as if at a private screening of her favorite picture show and I stood Silent and Golden by the door until she had replaced the dark brown burnt sienna pleated paper and set the box back down under the tree.

I do not always choose the truth, either. Perhaps hers was the mincemeat that kept some orphan hope or some blind couch critter alive. After all it was Christmas Winthrop might come poking down the chimney to steal a catnap on the couch or to spackle the fire with a story or fill the shoes with some skittish or slithering surprise.

We aped Christmas without him; coins assumed their slots under the headachy incandescence. We took our places on the couch. My finger gleaned from the jagged edge of a fallen ornament the one drop of cheer; I licked it, terrorized by all that mattered, was cherished or loved. We sat around, six boxes marked XMAS, some missing, married, or dead; opening our presents, mewing like pregnant cats. Outside the pelt of freezing rain, the scratch of excitable puppies waiting to come in. Egg nog clogging our sinuses, we are not all here; we are weary and no one wants to get the door.

Thank you very much.

Boughs of holly fa la la.

And to you too.

Mother says where are my wings, has the harpist arrived, one more time: and we sit for last year's photograph, again.

Mother dried the wishbone on the windowsill with the five ripening tomatoes and before I left she said PULL and she smiled and said good luck with your interview, Mae. (if after all those years she moved one ant trap the whole colony would be without its primary food)

I liked it when she called me Mae.

Suicide on the Cellular Level

"And soon after Dr. Cohn
came, he rushed out to the phone,
and he dialed: DANton-ten-six-"

His head, hard-boiled, an egg in a swivel chair. His neck is reptilian and receding (I don't like his looks). He primes each page of the application with his official stamp of saliva. Otherwise, it appears, he cannot turn the page. He does this twitching happy rat's whiskers and snorting occasionally.

He is one of the 106 ice-cold isomers of the world. His atomic number is listed under Group VIII, the noble gasses, too combustible to exist, other than alone. He rules from an electron cloud, taking one application in 1000; states with zero percentage of error that I am sp^3 hybridized, a carbanion in its rapidly equilibriating conformation, not Ivy League cement.

-I will marry, sir, one of those glowing isotopes of uranium.

-We will live like man and wife, two homologues in a house.

-We will grow our children in a petri dish. (I have come armed with my best features; my bunghole is clean and an army of chinese has pressed and repressed this skirt. Now, then. My mediocre MCATs.)

-I assure you, sir, I am not in that percentile.

-The questions, sir, were hard to understand.

-The girl behind me, sir, with her bubble gum.

-My lousy grades sir: remarkable, considering.

-The circumstances, sir.

-That I did not attend class.

-Awoke to find an insect in my bed, sir, *the nature of which I did not understand.*

-Flunked that lab practical, sir, because I could not identify the speared organ, because you see, I could not find, sir, the genital opening of the female crayfish near the third walking leg.

-I think some asshole yanked it off.

-Then I saw it, sir—two halves of a worm—inching away. I named it *Annelida* for worm only to see it fly away the order *Lepidoptera.*

-Why, I left the empty spaces blank and got the question wrong.

-I did not get credit for the question.

-His prejudice not neutralizing over time, I told him there are as many words for penis as there are for man.

-I got the F.

-I cried home to mother.

-You must tell the headmaster first, dear, that it is a duck, and then that it is a mallard and afterwards, if he should like to hear it, that he wobbles when he walks.

-But flight comes first! Motion, next. (Deer waiting at the sign to cross—I've not seen it.)

-All of my malignancies, sir, grown from innocent moles.

-A grandfather dead, sir, at the ripe age of 21.

-Sir, I have gotten so small as ten to the minus seven in joules and beyond.

-I have learned about ergs, sir.

-But I was—young and—again, the girl with her pink—Bubblicious—yes, that was it, that was the year I slugged myself with a six-pack and squatted over the interstate until I had nothing left to give. My hot piss, of course, steamed back at me, and I got sick and tired of smelling it but it's a long story, sir, and by the end of the semester I aim to be in the realm of the purely biological.

-Lub Dub.

-Lub Dub.

Negative infinity a quantity I've often contemplated, sir.

-Mount the malignancy on the slide, sir, to the tenth power of ten.

-Smell my fingers, if you like, sir.

-An English major, sir, but I can explain.

-I assure you, sir, four summers at the Cyanotics Institute cured me of that. (You trace over your face like an ouija board, doctor, as if you knew!)

-I am not the aesthetic butterfly that flits about, sniffling and sighing in some paperthin melodrama; confetti flakes, a small child's oragami. I have given up the bonehead english, sir. I'm one of you.

-I have opened up! Into thorax and abdomen! You are the stake that shoves me, drops me into the collection box, calls yourself an entomologist. Take that! Give it to me doctor! Subphylum: Mandibulata! Class: Insecta! Order: Lepidoptera!

-I'm no artistic archangel! I'm no aesthetic arse! We are, er, etymologists, here! *Trained* in the taxonomy of bugs!

-William Carlos Williams, sir, a metaphysician, like myself.

-The poem about the wheelbarrow, sir.

-Just a wheelbarrow, sir.

-A kind of homeostasis, scientifically speaking, sir.

-Time is not there yet.

-Well then, minimax: the minimus of a set of maxima.

-Yes, sir those are the facts.

-All of them, sir.

-I am sure, sir.

-Yes, oh *sir*! The very question! When I found Science, it was beautiful sir, I must tell you, allow me, sir yes! And suddenly my mind was a flurry of the most extraordinary biological facts all the mitigating factors of my life came to me all my questions answered: No wonder pee smells like ammonia. It is! It's NH_3! It is! And here's why H_2O boils fast on a mountain: $PV=nRT$! Whee! If I may, sir: why, everything I saw, I knew! The facts, sir: Perseus slew a small hydrozoan jellyfish. Medusa her name. Now here's why I can jump into the comb jellies off the pier: Kingdom: Animalia. Subkingdom: Metazoa. Phylum: Ctenophora. Now I know! Now I know! They don't sting! They don't sting! No *cnidoblasts*. I feel like one of the yachts, sir! I feel like one of *you*!

-Inertia: what keeps the frog from sitting up. (named my frog Sir Prufrock, sir, all pinned and wriggling: my first real operation)

-I knew it was meant to be, sir, when I looked into that frog and saw 200 miles of eerie intestinal loop de loops. Wow! Those pent up hands of mine, doctor! They kept shaking!

-He shat fecal bubbles on his way out, sir: we all do. Must have been an awful scare, they stink; I touched one.

-Again, the girl behind me with her bubble gum.

-My grandfather, sir, dead.

-My grandmother, sir, beastly funny as well.

-Phosphenes: the lights you see when you close your eyes real hard.

-Lysosomes: organelles that self-consume. Interesting concept, sir. Suicide on the cellular level.

-Don't you think?

-Sir?

-You can check the periodic chart, if you don't believe.

-I have balanced the chaste books of the molecular underworld and proved that you are my granddaddy and the father of my father.

-A brilliant essay, sir. I implore you to take another look. Stoichiometry and Religion; well, sir, both moths and butterflies are the Order Lepidoptera—in all due respect, I believe you mistook a colon for an unshared pair of electrons. An easy mistake to make.

-Surgeon's hours? Yes, sir! Up half the night junked on adrenaline (the LSD of words).

-Since epiboly, sir. Since the onset of gastrulation, I knew.

-And before! During tetrad formation, crossing-over, recombination. Every meoitic division! Every germ layer knew! And throughout lactation.

-I am told, sir, that at 3 cm. ossification begins.

-It's a dirty business, doctor, I know: Teacher pulled a brain (H. Sapiens) right out of a pan; must have been kind of embarrassing for the old corpse who spent four years at Harvard. Some psych major blew chow.

-Oh no, of course not sir, life makes provisions for those of your class, rank, and alma mater. The med students were fine.

-To drive the Porsche, sir. Scream nigger and fat man and frog! Everyone claims to have lived on my block. Everyone!

-Yes, sir! Quite the humanitarian, as well. Hovering over that frog that last afternoon with my scalpel and wits (well there she was again, snapping and waxing) and first I covered his legs with a paper towel and next I told him, you know, Sir Prufrock, your legs are a delicacy in some circles.

-He twitched, doctor, he did.

-Yes, a huffy voice that said, go ahead, eat it darling, it tastes like chicken.

-First I made a fu manchu of the paper towels and then I pinched myself, doctor, real hard. C'mon, it's true. Sir Prufrock has passed away in dissection.

-My life passed before me. Like a wheelbarrow, sir, meant to be discovered only once, each time. A frozen shutter, yet it was moving! And so I cried, aloud:

We shall never see each other again.

We shall never have that cabin together.

Death creeps.

Come to me, my love.

-The very thought of it, sir, crept up my tit like a goosebump and I ran! So much violence in the laboratory! Something always sitting up! But I returned, sir, here I am.

-Hobbies? Lots! I've got microfilm and microfiche; can trot a horse, milk a moo, macrame and tae kwando, bocci and ben wa, hoola hoops and chains; whipped cream and wafers, body and blood; been educated, masturbated, vaccinated, been depressed repressed obsessed possessed; know sundalini kundalini hari kari red rover bend over; the heimlich maneuver the butterfly flick; perpetual volunteerism unparalleled patriotism unprecedented donorism—my eyes and kidneys to the AMA.

-My clitoris and Grafenburg Spot to Masters and Johnson (right off the physiograph, sir!)

-Humor, Mr. Halitosis, sense of.

-12-24-36, sir, a perfect Erlenmeyer flask.

-Once a month my endometrium sloughs off.

-A woman, emphatically yes! I was lucky, sir. After years of vicarious and masochistic yearning I was instructed to take a handmirror with me to a warm bath. And there you have it, small and delicious, one of those dark sweet peanuts you pulled every sixth or seventh peanut from the shell; the pearl slobbering at the center of a slobbering sea membrane.

-The moment was preceded by a moment of defiant terror and of stillness.

-Yes doctor, I did.

-And when I became a woman for the first time it was like finding Science again oh yes I slid down that treacherous slide of lava and mud and ash, erupting, emptying all my grief and all my guts; and it seemed that for the first time I was not the natural wonder but Helena herself, naked and molten and existential, angry and excited, and that I could go on forever, pouring down that mountain, paw after thumping paw.

-Yes, in a paroxysm of athleticism and eroticism I became the woman I was.

-Oh Doctor!

-Sir?

-I do, sir.

-A life worse than celibacy, sir.

-I can, sir! I grow old before you and uppity and starched, a stoic mess, some pigeon-toed receptacle of brains.

-I promise, sir. I will forget to exercise. These thighs will rub and blubber against a sweaty nylon mesh. You'll see.

-They will call me tubby and triglyceride. No man will marry me.

-Barnum's Fat lady, sir, has missed her train.

-Children? Sir! The mention!

-The chemical name describing a bovine NADP-specific glutamate dehydrogenase contains 500 amino acids.

-3600 letters, sir! Who needs *mothers*?

-I will keep from pulsing forth, extract all emotion from my—autonomic nervous system—swallow all urges and drives, remain imperceptible and contained, execute exquisite control—of my adrenal—medulla.

-I have no left brain activity, sir, I swear.

-No sensation below the belt.

-Nonewhatsoever.

-My mansion waits for me with its silent butler and a dumbwaiter.

-My patio is a scene for raucous suburban laughter. (Like you I have cultivated a lawn of virulent phages and cloned the ones most like myself.)

-I can lick at my wine with perfect confidence (knowing what the peasants squish between their toes).

-I have skinned a yellow formaldehyde rat. Just peeled him back, two rawhide flaps. I am a scientist: I am!

-I am meticulous in expression.

-I will pinch the nurses and scold the rest.

-I am fit to operate.

-I trust you will put in a killing word when the committee convenes, sir. I trust, sir, that justice will prevail.

Forgive me, sir, but what are they like? Do they clip their toes and store them in a bedside urn marked Oomphala?

-Tell them I wear my orange ambitions around the corners of my mouth like a goofy moustache (Do you like me Hal, do you do you do you)

-Tell them I am tripping over myself, Hal, some fool's oversized shoes, honking my gazoo like some clown whose nose is insipid and lit.

-I beg you, sir.

-Sir I have already bought the sphygmomanometer; my ears ring like valves. Sloshing with the sound of inner organs and the telephone.

-I have Avogadro's number. (Visad was homesick; he was from India.)

-Check the EKG, doctor; it means a lot to me.

-My white squeegies, doctor, I'm wearing them, in difficult-to-find half sizes.
-My beeper, sir, here on my belt, where it is digital and glows.
-Ready and waiting for the whole world to hemmorhage in my hands, sir!
-Spent my days sterile and in isolation!
-March lst sir?
-Is that the fiscal or the academic year?
-I'll sleep by the door.
-Pavlov's dog.
-Just a scrap, sir.
-A scratch or a sniff.
-I'll jerk up from my dreams, sir. (oh, it's not on the resume, sir: odd jobs and sweet nothings for me own grandmammy rotting in the Irish death upstairs)
-6.023 x 10^{23} doctor!
-The scenario is right, doctor. I can tell!

When March arrives I take a trip, go to New York, buy myself a shotgun and a loft. Drop the nail in the soup. Rebuild Dante's inferno, stoke the fire where the bums keep warm. Don't mind me, bums, I tell them, I'm just one of those educated fellas second oldest after Harvard having a real whirl. (They had a certain reticence, were taut about the mouth and lips; they oppressed you with their knowledge. They were meticulous in expression.) A procession marches by—urban blacks in jack-up jive—flapping their sashes of one-upmanship; yo; immigrant families swoon and the Grand Marshall yips. Some majorette in nude pantyhose flips her baton to the passing cars and it is me.

Portrait of a Girl

(If I do it in daylight in daddy's garage some shithead coroner will screw up the autopsy and claim I died of natural causes.)

I have left the room/ where scientists come and go/ pithing Michealangelo

Remembering, sir, the one drop of epinephrine that kept that frog alive.

I believe in the truly altruistic, Herr Doktor, and my muse is no small/ white/ mouse.

? may a moody baby doom a yam ?

"'Nurse,' he said, 'it's an appendix!'
(In the middle of one night
Miss Clavel turned on her light
and said, 'Something is not right!'
Little Madeline sat in her bed,
cried and cried— her eyes were red.
And afraid of disaster)"

-A pelt made into a swivel on the top of an egg.
-Your toupee sliding off is all.
-Forgive me.
-That moose on the wall, doctor, yours?
-The deer and the antelope too?
-And a bloody good shot you are, doctor!
-A bit of the old all-or-none principle, I'd say.
-Can't refute the facts, sir.
-Two lumps, doctor, if you get around to it.
-A man should be proud.
-And if it weren't for the red neural splotch of chicken
in the scrambled eggs, I'd be all right.
-As for me, you realize, doctor, the plumb does not point
to earth center.
-That's why we're here, old sport.
-Yes well she's a big one doctor you with your six guns
and she with her two big bonkers.
-Have you no children?
-Not so close to my face doctor.
-I can see them from here.
-I prefer the Benzodiazepines. Barbituates or alcohol
will do.

-Now, then. How do you want the questions answered, left to right up or down back to front a show of hands how many fingers?

-It just washed up on the beach, doctor, vast and white.

-I do not understand distances greater than a mile or less than an inch. The good ship Lollipop has run aground. Or it might have been a quail egg, I don't know.

-I know it is difficult to tell magnitude under such bright lights and in such discrete quantities but how sick *am* I?

-Do you accept for pay bangle bracelets or commemorative coins?

-And if I were to say fettucini alfrrredo would that suffice?

-What do you use for game?

-Excuse my impertinence doctor but that there is a horse.

-Blinded by a little boy and put to sleep. I see.

-And is he OK now?

-And the boy, sir, who has the head of the boy?

-Doctor I feel this sickening sense of remorse and longing not afterwards but while there is still time. While I am still here.

-I went to the two-star motel and that's all I remember. Going into the bathroom to have a baby. Eating discarded nuclear material. Hangers soldered to the back of the closet, the bulrushes full. If that's what you want to know.

-The maids did me with the feather duster.

-A thong did not divide two globes and from the front their bosoms were not round and pert and held up by two generous hands.

-Dust to dust, that's all I ask.

-An antihistamine, doctor, would be fine.

-It all started sir the one summer I got stung by the bee.

-Attended by a bumpkin doctor who checked my reflexes only.

-Won't you need a buccal smear or two?

-My handkerchief?

-A pap, perhaps?

-Go ahead, doctor, it tastes like chicken.

-Is that the broncholator dilating doctor, or is that you?

-A few units of blood?

-I implore you, doctor, I have reason to believe there are—insect parts—open it up. Take a look. Oh I don't know—thorax or abdomen.

-Amniocentisis. I'm kicking for two.

-A horse of course.

-Could be you.

-I'm sure I acquired the rhesus factor with it.

-Snuff the little neuroblastomer.

-If she cannot count the permutations on her fingers I cannot help her.

-It was a wasp, sir, that stung me. My apologies to the bee.

-I awoke to see her—Phosphenes—from my pew. I tried to get the bloody netting off my face.

-Spiders in my scalp, that's a symptom, isn't it doctor?

-The stinger, I'm afraid, is still in.

-Feel for lumps.

-Feel for breasts.

-Too late for that?

-The formation of buboes?

-A dug or two.

-Help yourself, doctor. One lump would be fine.

-Use your Doppler Detector.

-The other one, doctor, just to be sure.

-What do you think of when you think of bratwurst. Freud a good answer! But the wrong one, doctor; I had Hitler in mind.

-Shall I say cheese?

-Which way to Rome?

-Are they malignant doctor?

-Thank you, *sir*!

-You have the kind embroidered face of a Sunflower, doctor, inlaid in yellow ruffles. Why with all the killing kindnesses leaning over me I'm not sure whose eye to roam. Hanging over my head the HOME SWEET HOME, a smiling coriander spoon; your office is a country kitchen, and I am in it.

-If only he owned a rathskeller, doctor, I would not be here. I would have fired the Stationer and written monkish poems instead and drank dank ale by the crested ponymug or rewrote the Dictionary.

-My shrunken pineal gland; howsomever, no longer responds to the Cape light.

-The basil leaf, doctor. Put it in.

-Calcium, then.

-I shall allow myself to be slowly laminated or endoscoped or rocked to sleep.

-Two sisters from fog harbor, Maine.

-Morphine would do.

-Ten days penicillin (imagine! in memorandum: mother of the mold!) before the low grade infection turns to inflammatory disease or ties my tubes.

-My stomach pumped, mouth washed out with belly of the dove, training school for boys—or girls—

-Shall I consult the personal ads?

-A little something for the binge-purge?

-Fettucini alfrrredo?

-Mother's spaghetti.

-Is it ptosis doctor (sagging or prolapsing organs)?
-A kind of increasing entropy?
-A pamphlet on schizophrenia?
-I live alone.
-Gangrenous?
-Nothing would surprise me, sir; I once had my brachial artery snuffed by a nun.
-Compulsive and indiscriminate, yes.
-Here are her two fangs.
-I have irreconcilable differences, true.
-If you have the Chinese boxes go ahead, sir; I shall try to get out.
-Sawed in half I am sure to extricate in one piece.
-Born with the umbilicus wrapped around the neck I was sent to the School for the Intellectually Challenged.
-Then, I was artificially inseminated by the nun.
-I hear that the rage in the Rockies is throwing frisbees to the dog for hours before supper. Shall I go?
-What I want, sir, is to be confident and fresh. I need safe feminine deodorant protection.
-Industrial Strength.
-A safari hat like yours. To belong to the Kenya Club.
-Do not send me to a horticulturist I do not believe in them.
-My grandfather was a landlubber, you know.
-Some seminiferous chortling in a terrarium, now and then.
-(Put a garter snake in a gasbag and tickled her little motor end plates pink.)
-I do not order endoskeletons Out or soft shell crabs just the same or kill my food necessarily before I eat it.
-A dab of zinc oxide and I will watch the pool.
-A lackey, sir, what I meant by the calcium.
-The Dow Jones Industrial Average, doctor, what is it?

-No, calcium is for the dowager, sir.

-Dragging a crooked hump, hurriedly along.

-Sometimes I am coquettish and sometimes I am brackish or fresh.

-Them voices coming out of a Woeman aren't all soprano, doctor. Some are plain ugly.

-Sounds like Grant's tomb.

-The embolism, doctor, the peanut!

-Yes, sir. A dowager.

-That is how I see myself.

-Slouching. From Bethlehem, or any other.

-Your breath packs a wallop, doctor, from across the room.

-Torah, Torah.

-Both how I see myself and how I am.

-Can you fly your white coat up onto the antler rack or make him blink from where you're sitting? Can you wiggle your big toe or does it do it on its own?

-I sometimes swear, more often to myself than aloud or to my mother. But I am working on it.

-Corned beef and cabbage and obvious debris I push to the side of my plate.

-Ouiiiiiii

-Why, it is a test of the emergency broadcast system doctor.

-Listen to what I just said.

-What do you think?

-Bellevue is no picnic but their poems are awfully good.

-I know for one I could never floss every day.

-Nor jingle the bed as often as I should like, without the sudden dispatch of orderlies and guards, or the howling and scratching alacrity of the others.

-Commemorative coins, doctor, do you take them?

-Unlike the others, I save the first polar body and kill the rest.

-My firstborn. I would name him Benjamin, doctor.

-Son of my right hand.

-Then I have Dexter.

-And on and on.

-Until every downcast bedlamite has broken its restraints.

-I'm worth my weight in bullion, doctor; a face not unlike the others.

-Never catching on.

-Doctor I've tried phenol red, the acid-base indicator, the home pregancy kit, pricking my finger; tweezers and fat calipers, ultrasound, the back of a brush.

-A blow to the head.

-I still name my children before I have them.

-I've gotten so beastly fat.

-Beastly, doctor, as in *dead*.

-Poofed like an Eclair.

-A much diminished vital capacity.

-My *word*, doctor, Read your *classics*!

-Everything shakes or jiggles, like my beached fat I suffocate innocent things and am acted upon by the cruelty and divestiture of others.

-All stomach; soufflé.

-I wear my clothes sloppy or nondescript.

-I am obligated to put my first foot forward and I dream.

-Like a bag lady my clothes are not rotted into me and you can tell.

-I drink too much and punish myself with long periods of abstinence.

-It's not easy being an athlete trapped in a fat lady's body.

-Diet? Sir!

-If I should diet I should deprive myself of comfort, become cranky and swollen, lapse into some vapid or middle class disease.

-I should like to fast—to sit in the lotus position—become philosophical and profound, instead.

-The fat are cynical, doctor.

-The sedentary, irreligious.

-I am not that fat.

-What religion are you?

-What with this godless existence of mine I thought I believed in desperation.

-I have stood before the automatic teller and over the toilet bowl, begging for mercy.

-With overwrought emotions and a slack face. Asking the same question.

-Three lemons in a row. Coming up. The coins. Rushing out.

-Insufficient funds.

-In the morning there was a little debit by my account.

-I have come here of my own volition.

-I guess you could call me a shell of a former self.

-Maybe I have entered what my father called the real world.

-Have you a riding crop?

-The failure of the imagination to bear arms.

-To pay the rent.

-I need something in my mouth: polyps, dollops, a bolus.

-Have you a peppermint, doctor?

-A little salt peter. Sugar, then.

-Two humps or one?

-Thirsty, doctor, is all.

-Arabian or Bectrian—

-Doctor if you cannot understand me how can you hope to win the war?

-I'll dry up and die against the wall of your tack room with the others.

-Should you choose to inject truth serum into me doctor would you be so kind as to ask first.

-If mother she had a matching tortoise bag or a terrapin purse—that is off limits, out of the question.

-If you decide to plant the electrodes in my pleasure center doctor I think that we should part better friends.

-Yes, I trust you, doctor, but not completely.

-Mother is the only one you can trust up your ass with a rectal thermometer.

-Put that in the Ledger.

-And father, too.

-The truth? No, doctor, some of it is a dump of lies. But it feels good telling it.

-So be it! For this is ordained: only one in twelve is telling the lie.

-Apostles. I sometimes wonder about the hairy paraphernalia on your growing walls.

-Doctor? I should like to retract that final dispensation from Rome.

-I was just mentioning, doctor, how nice you look in your yellow leisure suit.

-First thing I remember, some gargoyle leaning over the crib calling me names.

-Darling.

-I would tell them: Darling? I am not your darling.

-No, but I had rows and rows of stalactite gums.

-I loved it when they called me darling, doctor.

137

-Do you love it when they call you doctor?

-And my own personal favorite was baby tuckoo.

-Because he was already beastly famous in the crib.

-And soon speaking German as well.

-All my one-liners from the crib—some recent ad lib.

-A bit guilty about not being bilingual at that stage in my life, as well.

-"Slip into your sleepy-suit, my pretty one, it's time for bed. Time to dream my dreams."

-But I could smell the booze on the giant's breath. Jolly. Green.

-Look! Company! (it was not said): In the corner of the crib she masters her Mattel busybox. (A whorleyboid instead to launch and land from the pad of my embattered crib was out of reach and I was given a bowwow, bilious orange with a bow, as a clutchtoy instead.)

-The baby's not drinking the baby is dreaming your dreams. The baby can smell the booze on your breath.

-And soon I have a pet dog who receives commands to kill from jesus too. An Irish accent, as well.

-Spending nights alone, building molecular models, balking at company with one fine shrill while practicing *Worcestershire* in a particular corner of my crib.

-"Last time to replicate the family DNA, offer your strand to the double helix, darling, pass on the name of Watson and Crick to the next generation of dreams."

-I put it in some green crinkyl in a corner.

-We only suffer once. Then we turn around and go the other way.

-The palindrome syndrome.

-To this day, one who says Darling! I cannot meet with equanimity, just angst.

-I said bad doggy *bad bad* so that I might live.

-Mother? Not to blame. She changed me regardless. Mammals and marsupials alike.

-She always said *Yum Yum* when she wanted me to eat. Sometimes *Num Num* when she herself had things to do or wanted me dead. (And as for him: no again; daddy's shirttails hanging out propelled our kites across the lawn little running legs to catch him when he's home.)

-Then it was lights out (has everyone seen the baby) and some Brobdingnagian leans over my crib and belches his beer and offers to change me.

-I screamed bloody murder, doctor, about all I could do. (I knew then the novel was not my best event.)

-Others came into the nursery to fix their hair.

-Emptying the whole contents of their purses onto the changing table.

-Oh—the hard knob of a cervix, a couple of frayed tubes, ovaries rolling around like marbles on the bottom. Some miscellaneous tissues I couldn't identify (but I would, doctor, years later).

-I barked and they disappeared into the belfry to do the rest.

-Two boys two girls and myself.

-Me and sister were such charges in our sleep. Piping up from the dark, doctor, we would ask the same questions, in fact, you are asking!

-Which would you rather be: deaf dumb paralyzed.

-I always took deaf. (it would be too big for the tub in 3 months and then where would they put it)

-Would you have chosen dumb, doctor?

-Sometimes we squeezed our eyes shut and said the same word over and over until we got it right; a me a me a *me*.

-But it was never really *me*. Like I would have said it if it were really *me*.

-Then father poked his head into our room and said *no monkey business.*

-Yes I miss getting my pajamas on. All the production and protocol at bedtime.

-Pillow fights. Feathers flying.

-Never spent a night without her in the next bed.

-The rest of them, either.

-We played outside the laundry vents and then I heard the clanging.

-Since then I really haven't slept a night in my life.

-Sir would you kindly have a breathmint.

-It's been two weeks now.

-Doctor?

-I told you father always spackled his face with a bit of blood before he arrived at the breakfast table.

-Have I told you that?

-Not true.

-Confetti as far as I know.

-I learned my capitols off a placemat at Hojo's.

-We played the license plate game, too, begging father to overtake the turkey trucks rattling to their destinations; it was a thrill, with the lurch of his big shoe, I admit, to find Alaska first, but it didn't always happen.

-Well I wasn't going to ax the family, if that's what you mean.

-They took us to Disneyland. We saw a bear jamboree.

-The standard fare diving and flaming through hoops.

-The truth, doctor. I saw the talented young porpoises and wanted some day to jump dauntless through the fringes, too.

-I had no patience for the zany dancing bears; no, I would have rather played hangman on the way to Seneca Falls, doctor, but I didn't complain.

-Oh yes and a seal balancing a ball we saw.

-Oh the way back and a dog nodding its head in the back of a car.

-We were tailgating, I admit.

-I am not defensive doctor.

-I wasn't driving.

-Sticks and stones, doctor.

-Doctor are we there yet?

-In fact, sir, it comes to me now, after all these years, vertigo. Carsick. *Watching the bouncing* (hushpuppy) *dog*.

-Doctor, I'm good with an ax, but Lizzy Borden I'm not.

-A Raskolnikov of sorts. The perfect crime. No apparent motive. The mind.

-A conscience doctor? That's when you hear your father's voice 27 years later when he is no longer in the room.

-Yes and when they took us to San Francisco, they pointed first to two fags, then to Sausilito and then to Auschwitz (Alcatraz, was it).

-I liked the fags better than Athens, too.

-I had a greasy eyeball, always looking for some infraction. Though I was quite taken by the Sphinx.

-Two girls two boys and me.

-I told you that.

-The only one stuck in her terrible teens.

-I am the only begotten poet, doctor, ginseng at best.

-Toothless twin, grinning grin.

-Sensible she was, a sense of sadness and resignation beyond her years.

-Common sense.

-I sometimes disturbed the sleepy hollow of her reading—*Madeline*, the pious girl with the towering siesta hat; somber impressionist background against the girl. The girl she took out every night to read, the girl I should have been, the family aficionado, the good sister. The nun.

141

-Madeline, stuck bristling in her side of the closet under the Chinese doll I scalped for spite.

-Oh, I preferred a mad mop the color of Pippi Longstocking, sir, whom I long venerated for her sterility and hilarity, as well as her impromptu adventures on the high seas.

-I fixed her train up on the altar and carved back the years with a putty knife, hiding my face in the fishnet mantilla saying *Worcestershire, Worcestershire.*

-Smearing frosting on my own faces, burying the tiny pitchfork faces of the nuptial couple in the bottom tier of the cake.

-Stepping on the family feet.

-Making plans for the future.

-Mother said something old something new.

-Yours only to hold.

-Someone cuts in to borrow the bride.

-"Pretty to look at
 Nice to hold
 If you break it
 We mark it *sold.*"

-A knickknack shop, doctor.

-A proprietor to the groom.

-For a sloe-eyed groom to honor and obey.

-I went to the bed of the sleeping Madeline and told her what I'd seen: I even picked out—our Oneida flatware—our pattern in crystal, I even bought the gravy server; it was half-price.

-Stuck to the brooding promises I made at make-believe. I could only ape this wedding. A way of life.

-I am not doing some silly renegade dance with father, he is spanking me over the bed.

-Carving my own cake. I took thee to be my whole wedded life: my consummate glow! little sister! conjugal

twin! (who caught the booger on the nose and made the promises only I could keep.)
-Growing old without her.
-Perhaps it is I who is Madeline and the somber impressionist background which has usurped the girl.
-I am left dancing with the Michelin tire man.
-Liar.
-The hunchback on the chocolate cake, have you fed her?
-(And yes I wish she were there to fart at my wedding.)
-I might commit in one rash inexplicable act the silence she spent years pruning.
-I think she is hiding somewhere in this room doctor; my eyes cannot work the peripheries fast enough, though it was I who did the hiding.
-I cannot remember her nom de plume; I listen for the battering slats of her eyes.
-And in one of those arch resonating laughters of our childhood together I sprung forth, she called me by the wrong name.
-Watch it!
-Doctor!
-Boo!
-Some aunts screeched who catches it will be next!
-(I am busy fixing daddy's cummerbund.)
-It is I who feel awake in bed, this empty darkness jumping out.
-Like an earwig, doctor, I am moving sideways fast.

-I don't know German sir but they call her the führer.
-She said *passion* like *daschund* doctor.
-I saw the limesalts and stalactites, and I freaked.

143

-Then her eyes tapered and she went tsk and too bad and poof!

-Liar! Doctor! She did not go poof! Just like that.

-That's a whole 'nother story. (My rainy day billets-doux. Some odd crushes. Some unnatural daydreams.)

-*Th—Th—Th—milieu* she said, like a frenchman says, peu, peu.

-She was often drunk when she said it.

-She did not say *you*, doctor; *yeu* she said *yeu*.

-She did not bonk me three times with her wonderwand she did not leap up and tap her hightops twice or thrice. She had masterful verbs, silver slippers, and a vertical jump.

-She was no dyke doctor, if that's what you're after.

-Normal in that respect, sir.

-Nothing touches me that turns me to stone.

-I am Pavlov's dog.

-I am classically conditioned.

-It is only important that they eat their eggs al dente, doctor.

-She said, "Yours til caviar lays its eggs sweating and grunting."

-Perhaps she said "ta ta."

-God knows, she left.

-You know those fairy types, doctor, they always deliver their proverbial punchlines before they poof!

-Sir, ask the questions!

-The question is, sir: she would not submit to a mammogram and why.

-I'm telling you sir, under the cushions. Gum!

-The freaks of love.

-Kate Millett and her beloved Sita handpicking their vegetables at the open air market.

-Vladimir and his lolita pup.

-Mailer's Marilyn in lipsticks and wigs.

144

-The Sisters Brontë riding sidesaddle alone.

-The tumor was malignant doctor.

-The right one.

-I was almost there, too, doctor.

-She knew the mischievous Heathcliff would come.

-Because she could not stop for Him / He kindly stopped for Her.

-The right tit, doctor, more precious to her than life.

-It was good for me too.

-She slackened opened stiffened subsided. Like all the summers of my life.

-While it lasted why I suppose now she is fanning herself in the shade of the polite euphemism we all share.

-Death, doctor, what I mean.

-I am like Stephen Dedalus in that respect, sir. I neither believe nor disbelieve.

-Neither casually heterosexual nor needlessly homosexual.

-I am neither.

-I read somewhere the artistic temperament it is androgynous.

-Scared, doctor? I am the cold-blooded coed who humped the sick.

-First I stabbed her and then I cried: "Don't die."

-She begged. She died. I saw her eyes.

-Perhaps I am the molten pile you call her spell.

-I have buried myself in a crypt of her favorite things, kiwi dolls, acrylic tile, heiroglyphics.

-Voodoo, doctor, do you believe.

-I put the spell on myself reading into it the aztec indians.

-I do not fear Geronimo like I fear being bedridden in my golden years with a laconic spouse.

-I would rather watch my secretary eat his lunch.

145

-Not all secretaries are as you think, doctor!

-Not all secretaries are women, either, sir, for what it matters to you.

-Why must I prove one to get to the other.

-There was the homesick Visad; he was from India; I invited him up.

-He looked up at me like a giant loom.

-He was looking for his mother.

-Clearly, I was not his beloved Calcutta.

-There was a Svede named Oaf with his blond looks and his delivery boy style.

-He was a scatterbrained goat with creamy buttermilk skin, and his jangling, boyish approach would get our fisticuffs started by bucking articles from the desk and chewing the furniture.

-Oaf, as far as I know, doctor.

-I did not want his children.

-Though I fail to see how saying it will keep me from doing it again. (The little wrangler had a sticky milkweed kiss and grazed all day on flecks of paper from the *in* and *out* box of my desk.)

-I am needlessly terrified, doctor, knowing he was no simple shepherd.

-The good poet Plath said they came to her in Ionic deathgowns, and they did.

-He is an eidetiker who knows my dreams, has an assistant in the human form, I am sure of it.

-He plunks things down on my desk to see how much I will eat.

-The meatcutters take me to their abattoir of swinging pink meats; it is a bucolic place with missing teeth. Olaf, they tell him, you can go now.

-A practitioner by the name of kiwi has a paper and a pen and speaks no english. She gets older every day but does not die. She is in the hooks for good, for one oriental lie.

-She knows god is killing her somewhere in eternity but does not know why.

-She does not seem to mind (what disturbs me).

-Why, I would rather, sir, tumble into the moat on the way in.

-I don't care to be found dead in the old house, dead for ten days, if that's what you mean.

-I do not wish to die of salmonella poisoning at a cat food convention out by the trash, either.

-I am crying, doctor: yes.

-Next week you must ask me about my grandparents and why.

-A cat named Bernadette saw them rising from the ashheap out at Lourdes.

-Hold my thumb, doctor.

-Down here, she said laughing, in the tuna melt! (some rice cake threw me in with the potted plants)

-My grandparents in the trashmasher. Still.

-The Molloy in me, doctor. Suck of stone.

-A taste in my mouth, doctor, have you a mint?

-Burnt mochoa moth, sir, as good as the next. The mint?

-In the city, sir, all children look like Buddy Hackett. They all have twisted tubular mouths.

-Next thing the old ones are sliding into a mash of something, kicking up.

-Can I tell you about my life as a puppy, happy, neutered, fixed?

-A scotchie would be fine.

-She doesn't see too well, doctor. Not without her goop glasses.

-I skinned a yellow formaldehyde rat and she said *good for you lady jane* (hippos have tiny birds to pick the parasites out of their eyes)

-She had cataracts, you know.

-I don't know about the birds.

-She had me, doctor.

-You have Eckelberg's eyes.

-What do you use as homing pigeons besides your horn rims? (The starlings are regularly spaced along a telephone wire; the boxer shorts hung just close enough to its wife's brassiere.)

-I use the sun as my compass, magnetic fields, and visual details.

-I am a scientist! I am!

-She was driven away in the back of a truck. Somebody threw me a monkey in the London fog and I asked him, looking back, could he play hurdy gurdy he said *no* but he could hold open that checkerboard cap if he could feed me bananas (that was the deal) but I did not look blind enough and he's still with me, chirping and shitting.

-If you must know, doctor. In the nutshell. It's all there.

-She looks up out of the trash now and again with the gobbling phosphorescence of a racoon caught in the act. The black stricken pinpoints of her eyes which is the exact locus of fright. The next generation looking on. A house of mirrors. The back of a broom.

-What I want to know—who has her icebox and shears, some cold-blooded coed like me? The boys of Lauderdale, they'll have me too, jingling back to the landfill (sealing for the mouth and eyes, covered with the ashen cloak and delivered by three stouts into the backend assup of a

venerable fifteen wheeler up with it! all aboard! heave! ho!
watch that step! handle with—dang! We're here. What's
that funny smell?)

-I am still unclear whether the moths have crumbled off
adobe walls or hatched from the powdery crush of malted
milkballs, leaving their semisweet cusps melting in the
mouths of maids, or right here in our hands.

-The two possibilities are to put it into words or to
remove it from the language altogether.

-But this is a fallacy because the vegetables are thriving
in a more or less state of intermediate consciousness, aren't
they?

-Like the leaning sunflower in your face, doctor, you act
as if you knew.

-How do you explain the rustling intervention from the
back of the truck?

-And who was that plutocrat in the dryer?

-And why does He come only on Fridays to this particular block and on Tuesdays or Wednesdays to the others?

Will those psychotic episodes by the pool, in church, at
home, in school stop; once I place the barrel at the foot of the
driveway in the middle of the week or remove the tinny lip
from the ear of the solid milk chocolate rabbit on Christmas; will I hear the crunch crunch of the Weltanschauuang
monster finally as it empties from its in situ position
Upstairs?

She left me her hot hand her skullcap and candle, her
giddy toot toot beamend behind, her dizzy notions her
spotty navy blue dress her cups and saucers; love, her
sublime bunny hutch.

I would have liked to have had my eggs hidden too but
the Easter bunny did not come to me in short white hairs
and gold trim. (It was a true story because mother always
told me when she was being facetious.)

Portrait of a Girl

I keep in a notorious pile by my crib some *green crinkyl.*

-Yes, and suddenly doctor I am no longer an artist or even an anarchist but so and so's secretary. I work for money. My dreams stink.
-Some silent indifferent third party has taken control of my life.
-Some indignant moral majority.
-Some third world Don Juan.
-All I can do is get drunk and swear.
-I had hoped to become one of the suicidal poets, sir. I had hoped to be dead or famous by now. But the shark in my blindspot, sir, it is still there.
-Could be anything.
-I told you doctor it is too curly.
-I wanted to do something, doctor, well you know, with my life, but all that came out of my mouth was someone else's problems (ich, ich, will not do black shoe).
-I might raise palominos or firedogs, open a spotlick cleaner, leak into the snow, play hackysack, oh I don't know.
-I suppose I could go on a fact-finding mission to the third world.
-Dr. Gravity's kite shop needs an apprentice.
-I could move to New York.
-Too old for the peace corps.
-Too old for the army.
-Maybe I'll get in, yet.
-I'll study medicine in the Caribbean. A casualty on the beach.
-Grenada or Guadalajara, then.

-Maybe like Nurse Nightengale I'll boil water for the chiefs of staff.

-Maybe like Clara Barton I'll be named after an exit on the New Jersey turnpike.

-Like Betsy Ross I could wait for the next state to secede into my lap.

-Maybe like Mary Magdalene I'll be named after a devout lawn statue.

-Maybe some day I'll wash up on the beach, a genie in a bottle.

-I could join the pop professions. I could be a gerontologist or a sanitation engineer; a hypnotist a lawyer an MSW; I could be a palm reader meter reader or sword swallower; paralegal parapsychologist or a massage therapist. An acupuncturist witchdoctor hoofer mouseketeer chiropractor a hoof and mouth doctor! An ear and throat man. Eight more years, doctor, and I could be you!

-Nostalgia that sickens me. Emotions that disgust me. Words that embarrass me. Parents I love.

-It's upper middle age and the center of the house is the bird feeder.

-Mother keeps saying the nuthatches are at the feeder, dear.

-Nothing pleases him.

-She still has the unbearable patience to iron.

-The scissors in the scissor drawer.

-There is much too much at stake to move on.

-It's a long tollroad home.

-They were supposed to be getting ready to trade three month's milk for a turn at the violin.

-Now this.

-They were supposed to have waited throughout the winter for this one day at the beach.

-The mallard mailbox where father is himself again, strolling out to check the rhododendrons.

-He cannot find the bone he buried thirty years ago.

-It is in the front yard somewhere.

-This depresses me.

-The furniture is covered.

-My mind a bust.

-Was I some geek who cleaned her plate lock, stock and barrel—for love?

-On Cape Cod they individually wrap your pickles in their own aluminum foil.

-It is the place to be for grandmothers, canning and jamming.

-A beached whale on the front page news every day.

-They are entitled to that.

-Weathervane and chimes. Fa la la.

-Puppies again. Happy, neutered, fixed. His dugs bigger than hers. All the old jokes turn on him.

-I can only dream, of angry cocks, black and big.

-They'll have to sell the house.

-Some things never change.

-So many of my friends are married.

-I name my children after the spices.

-After Marjoram and Paprika, I have Dill.

-I have stopped changing gears on my tenspeed.

-I make trips to the scissor drawer and back.

-Look for my keys. Plug and unplug the iron.

-Then I turned 27.

-Crawled away in a babble with the brain of a small animal.

-Mommy.

-Daddy.

-That's when I started this book.

-Holed up in my uncle's hotel.

-A dog's life.
-Next week.
-I concur.

-She is kneeling in the bathtub and her skin squeaks
and she is pink and sweet, buried in the jungles of National
Geographic bearing the world's last two surviving albino
monkeys. She looks up at me, doctor, some mangy creature
with prophetic eyes, and the dream begins.

She looks into the camera owning her own breasts
because she does not know it is a gunbarrel because the
man with the black box is not important to her because she
is alone in the room with her mother because her breasts
belong to her because it never occurred to her that millions
of Americans had captured her at this moment because no
one told her to smile because she was fay ray and because
she does not know he has x-ray eyes to see through skirts.

I am her mother, doctor, I cannot protect her from
stupid boys, old men, words like oompapa, bravo, mama
mia, olé, vive la différence or bon appétit. I cannot help her,
coming of age in the National Enquirer, whole city swallowed
by Giant Boob.

I am knocked up. With child. In my family way. She
is a bastard. She is a child. She is a girl. She is kneeling
in the bathtub and her skin squeaks and she is pink and
sweet as she asks the inevitable anatomical questions. The
engorged mushroom cloud, the tiny atom, how her whole
wide world got fucked into submission by a language that
mutilates and licks.

She looks for answers. I preface my remarks. It is a
strange upside down world, I tell her, rarely uttered but
understood. The Japanese take pictures and the nuns wear

bells on the points of their moccasins and try to make the pope laugh. It is a private place, I tell her (it is stupid, silly, ugly, stinks). Grudgingly, I teach her the language: her numbers 1 and 2; her birds and bees, storks and buzzards; the proud impossible rods and the snivelling stinkfish; the blindness and warts. Shall I begin with—the nice senso-receptors—the fine—bristlehairs? No.

I sacrifice dignity and discretion. Before someone pulls her aside, tells her of a curiously begotten son. I don't want her to wait for the school nurse, a Mrs. Ovum, the lampoon character with all the menstruating paraphernalia taking girls and boys silently aside, shaking her buttress behind, telling them of blond brains and blue balls. I do not want to wait until she is thirteen and her body no longer belongs to her; is wrested from her with wolfwhistles and innuendo, stares and subterfuge; the rheumy backwash of black men with mouths full of marbles. Rubber baby buggy bumpers; no, I will tell her. Read the words silently to yourself while mommy reads them aloud.

Cunt: The hole between a bitch's legs.

Snatch: Slang for above. Man-eater. Flytrap. Teething trapjaw snaps shut; needs to be taught a lesson.

Pussy: Nice little putty cat. Dumb silly animal. Does not take itself seriously, does not know its own name.

Vagina: Where babies come from. Where storks come from. Where the penis should have been. Where tampons are inserted.

Genitalia: Class intelligentsia. What the birdbrain taxonomist smears from the speciman in the stirrups. (And after Marjoram I have Genitalia stillborn.)

Pudenda: On the sex agenda; only your thesaurus and the flabby pointing arm of the school nurse knows. Buried in the Lexicon of Charlotte Emily and Ann; next to Death, Emily's only rhyming word.

Twat: Splat.

All I could think: ich, ich, will not do, black shoe. Again. Someone else's problems. She cannot refer to herself in public without trepidation, anger, shame, humiliation, inference, or analogy; without being silly, erudite, obtuse, obscene. History tells her, the text tells her, Abby and Ann will tell her; boys ejaculate, girls menstruate. That's why they took the boys into the other room—to tell you—you will squat to drop the berries and they will run around the house yelling Alyoop! (A woman is a castrated man. Men believe these things and children pick them up.) History writes off the entire female genitalia; nada, nothing, not there.

I point to it. Sea anenome. Squishy. Nietzsche. Jellyfish. Beat Meat. Silly Putty. Pud. Mud between the toes. A pleasant feeling. "Feminary," I tell her. (Some female authoress warrior feeling her oats in her brass bojangle beehive boobs invented that one.)

She looks puckishly at it and then at me. When the phone rings she puffs herself up like a blowfish.

I must leave her alone in the bathroom with that crude cuddlefish I have left waddling between her numbers one and two. The receiver smells of waxy buildup; it is blocked with the agglutinates of foul morning breath asking correct

155

time and the aspirated particles of Custodial telling me what he is doing to himself.

One moment alone in the bathroom some proselytizing stranger has taught my child to wipe her pink void cunt back to front; has flung open his man's monogrammed terrycloth robe and toilet trained my child, pointing to the crisp white ribbon stretched taut over his linoleum privy, telling her to wait, that she cannot begin officially this scenario, cannot snap this tape, must maneuver around it, praying not to spot it, must wait, instead, for He, himself, the mayor with his giant scissors, or the Japanese; or else he will grow silent and indignant, morose and impotent; we don't like to see him like that, we like to see his erection spring up, the bulbs flashing and popping; we must keep his throne immaculate, his seat up! Until it is time! Or death and damnation. People will talk.

At eleven as waxen as a string bean then musky pulpy smelling engorged.

Don't touch it! It is a place for which there are more euphemisms than death. (He likes to watch. When you bend over he is there with the split pea of your anus and he lingers to make sure. Don't bend over!)

Don't be surprised if some monastic bacteriophage injects you with the bombast and suds of his mousy brown DNA, his vittles and spots (These tender moments in the bathtub with my own child are pagan rites to an unmarried mother.) Don't let the reverend autograph your bible. Don't send for the ginsu knives. Don't touch it! Don't bend over! Don't be afraid to break the chain letter; do not dip blindly into the brown robed pot belly of the cookie jar it's Brother john!

(Ye pot smokers die of Paraquat all ye bumfuckers of Aids.)

We are not alone in this room; there are two toysoaps, a pair of cups plasticized in sterile isolation; a small shitstain on the inside bowl. Someone has gone and stuck a fragrance around the backside, probably a maid.

"Feminary," I find myself repeating myself unnecessarily, again. Does she see the one eye dilate and the other taper off as I speak remotely, painfully, and not of the thing itself but of the sickening truth? The soap is a slippery disk concave on both sides and twice it slinks out of my hand and rides the back curve of the tub. I swish the water, grope for words, (oh why haven't they left us a set of the plump ovals, oh why haven't they left us—the bellies of doves?)

Don't spend too long in the bathwater, I tell her. Wrinkles and prunes. I snatch a towel off the rack it looks like a bathmat, I can't tell, I press it into my face, it smells like the dry cleaners, like burnt terrycloth, like seared mothballs, like the sinuses of an old house, like TB, like a great aunt's decongestant—her nasal memorabilia—as she leans out the window to shake her geraniums; it smells awful but I keep on smelling it. No, it doesn't smell like any of that, it smells deadly, disinfectant, like chloroform. It saturates every linen here and every bug screwed into this room keels over in the belljar Fundamentalism. It may sit like baking soda in the back of the frigidaire but cannot fumigate the whole house or teach you things you cannot know.

I wrap the swaddling bastard XX christchild in the gauze by the bed palms pointed amen telling her she is lucky to have her sex mixed up somewhere in her guts she will never have to prove anything by machismo or mathematics (the slope of the forehead how close the monkey is to man) or twist the necks of chickens so men could be men. I look back into the mirror and ask myself, "Do you want to bring another child into this Bible Belt?"

Portrait of a Girl

Another question: where are the rich gifts you promised to bear? (Up to a full moon at noon. I grip the stirrups for something left to bear. A manuscript who screams my name.) She starts her flapping melodrama, only to be slapped. I slip her into her manilla skin, seal into her magenta folds.

She clamps me, pink and puckering, to her vacuous need to surge. (The good witch tittering from her chamberpot below, where she has spent her centuries Evil and on the rag.)

I try injecting the right words into the language but like the Susan B. Anthony dollar, never catching on.

Other children are called Ezekiel, Ecclesiastes, and Deuteronomy but they are children of Webster or of God. You are some Abortion.

We have as many words for whore as eskimos have for snow. But like my mother I teach my children to make their angels in the snow and when they are born first thing I ask them *do you like butter*? (Archimedes was in the bathtub already famous when he discovered his principle, too.)

Get your hands off your weiner.

This book is not about Bar Harbor Maine, doctor. This book is about the years I crossed off my calendar X by X trying to live my life. The spurt of an artery and the grub of the ever-inching worm: feelings.

I will not walk, scrubbed and dumb, clear at the throat, to the bed of my granddaddy. Tell him of malignancies I've named. I have chewed off that gristle; what to be and what to become. Where to end, and where to begin.

(How could I possibly find Poly-U if I couldn't even find the edge of the scotch tape.)

No, I cannot name that disease, but I can lean over that gray face and wail (a story that never ends)

I knew you would tell me to try the allied health sciences but I always wanted to return to Dublin or Yoknapatawpha County as the fat black lady on the maple syrup bottle.

You should have said: You were the little girl barred from the sacristy. God has never prevented you from doing what you could. But you did not.

(I drop one eye in a hypertonic solution and suddenly I can see myself on MTV rappin' and breakin' on my heliport. I wear earrings big as hoola hoops and like Leda I have my sunglasses on during the night and love who I am; when Zeus comes to me in the form of a swan I see the negative and not the picture.) My body arches to this nightmare. I must go on defying medicine, rejecting graphs of my own skin. Smell my children. Lick my lies. Make love to my hairy indecision.

I feel a bit of an accent coming on.

I drop my pagan money in the basket on a stick and move on.

Thank you, doctor, anyway. You gave me the strength of a man's antiperspirant. (Eloquence, doctor, a matter of putting the wrong words in the right place. I haven't any. Thank you very much.)

I don't mean to sound conceited doctor, but all my life I never felt understood.

I live here, doctor, amongst the infrared, because it is glowing. I draw my water from the well. Cool and clean as the knife. Poisoned or not, I drink it. Nowhere am I tacit or implied. It is my own world.

And when I die the life of my father passes before me and my mother agrees: *sit on a potato pan otis.*

(prove to me the consubstantiality of man and wife and

Portrait of a Girl

I will follow you anywhere)

Was it kind to its mother?
Did it speak to the cats?
Did its father wear army boots?

Bar Harbor Maine

"Miss Clavel ran fast
and faster,
'Good-bye,' they said, 'we'll come again,'
and the little girls left in the rain.
Madeline was in his arm
in a blanket safe and warm.
In a car with a red light
they drove out into the night.
(Outside were birds, trees, and sky—
and so ten days passed quickly by.
One nice morning Miss Clavel said,
'Isn't this a fine—
day to visit
Madeline.'"

I crept out of the Skinner box, daring to go blind: looking straight into the eclipse, without the adaptive eyepiece, precision angles, or design. Went to D.C. to finish *Ulysses* after 64 years. Like my neighborhood I underwent gentrification; calm and smug I moved in where I had toiled poor and honest in an angry sun. First day on the metro, Nietzsche handed me his card: deaf-mute. Can you help me?

He just stood there.

Jogging by the Aid truck parked at Peace Park dispensing beans and coffee to the nation's homeless, I reached out to touch one.

Maybe I would meet Mandingo too. Chained together to the wall of an English basement on U street; we would perform the grunts and animations while them whiteladys from Georgetown said some beautiful things.

I said to the fat black lady Yo County 1986: I am taking you to Dublin, my treat. She sat on the stoop across the street drinking her bag lunch, heading her extended black family (it was true they had names like Applejack and Buckwheat Okra and Sweet Potata Pie); she could have set for the maple syrup bottle; she was the southern black lady who stuffed jamstocks in masonjars; she still said hello (is that yer calica cat), and when she called her children I got hungry. (I ate couscous, hummus, gyros, and dora wat; ate with my hands, feet, and out of the well of my bellybutton.)

Who would have guessed that she would become the transparent starlet of my most ambitious novel to date? I think she thought I rather smelled like an owl exhibit.

The front stoop was a sublime place for the unemployed or for a writer to decide who was hanging right and who was hanging left. A good place to get blasted by the rain, to satisfy the imagination, take part in quiet irony or state of the art existential gloom. You could feed victuals or a bowl of souring milk to the yowling cats, eat a soda cracker, write doggerel, drink a beer, or disarm the passers-by.

One walked the streets, one thought for a thinktank downtown, one hung the upside down Peking duck in the Chinatown window. There was an enigmatic black family who built a fence around their car, boatpeople in a warehouse at the end of the alley we nicknamed the Mung, some dispassionate or surly black women who never said hello, black men puttering and spitting, yuppies walking yuppies, dogs and bagmen pissing and pissing into the alleys.

If you dared to stoop-sit, bitch alone, the black men stopped to serenade, clucking and kissing: bitch, you talkin' to me? Not to exalt their lassitude or indifference, you looked them in the eye, and then away; *yo*, bitch, *pussy*;

Thompson

followed by silence or extrapalatory comments by their
women and communal black whitepeople laughter.

(some shit stink and some shit don't) I guess they
thought I was Margaret Mead moving in to caress and
study the chimps. I got to know myself better in the
unwanted and vernacular. While they moved on, vomiting
their unimpassioned triumph over me.

But if like that swishy flamingo Lenore, iris of evening,
you cocked your chin and walked three Pekingese, your lies
understood, your breasts leavening over time, first faggot
to take the black drink, you might beautifully survive.

Well, you know, for the little girl banned from the
sacristy, it was heaven.

When the fat black lady had to get up, she looked,
perhaps, like she had eaten a ligonberry. She led with the
deformed crux of her hip, up one step and backing into the
house to change the channel on the TV (the silent arbiter of
her bustling innercity home). From across the street on a
small patch of astroturf I saw the whole cuisinart of elusive
household items. If I were Monty Hall I would give her $20
for every latchkey child in her changepurse. $50 for cats.

(I will pick Door #3 because behind Door #3 is the large
Yak nobody wants.) Dressed as Radish and Turnip, coming
from Dubuque, Osh Kosh, and Biloxi, they all want to plant
the kiss on the cheek of the one so holy. Monty Hall. The
Big Deal of the Day. (If she chooses Door #1, she will go to
Beulah's Beauty Nook for a hair weave. Door #2 and she
will be evacuated from in front of the tv (whole family
removed from one Room)). She just sits there, wetting and
mulching.

But the fat black lady herself usually said hello, and if
sometimes I met with cabalistic silence it was not uncanny,
it was left unsaid; we did not pretend to understand each
other completely but I believed we liked each other. She

greeted the topsy turvy cornucopia of my face, watched me
dispense victuals to the stragglers, too, and seemed to ask:
what I'm doing, a girl like me. I am writing a novel, I told
her (*black like me*). She said: I'm sure it's very good.

The cats went to her to express their innermost feelings. I think she was trying to say what some lady of color
some ego-tripping black poetess giovanni had said (nikki
her name): we can be comprehended only by our permission. (but it is my own nana soaking her psoriasis in the
tarbaths Upstairs while the fat black lady on the maple
syrup bottle watches closely Door #3) It was conceivable to
love them for their little blind afflictions or their one
dereliction alone.

The city nights reek of our Consummate Abnormality.
Scratching each other's crotches and eyes, sitting on the
front stoop, equivocating between Faith and Duty, we
survive: the school for artistes, e. coli and monkeys. The
Hollywood snuff film.

How inimically like the the eyeless fishes we have
evolved, tearing at our eyes with rags and turpentine. The
Easter bunny again; did not come to us in short white hairs.

Brutal blob, the human eye.

I had a black beau I called him my *main man*. I was
standoffish and he was a fox with a rip cord stomach. He
understood when I turned against him. After he seated me
I asked him how it felt to be the party of two. He gave a
scathing account of the back end of the bus and I told him
she was my hero, too, a Mrs. Rosa Parks from Rumford
Maine, was Betty Friedan his grandmother? I read Harriet
Tubman I believed myself hunted by the underground
railroad my favorite book was *Black Like Me*. He left lousy

tips and I was still flaunting my riches and championing the poor with my good credit.

All my life I had a secret caustic place in my heart for the retaliatory politics of Angela Davis and Malcolm X and I was betrayed by phlegmy black men who treated me like that, *pink chum* I told him: the last to allow me freedom or anonymity, much less advocate my *rights*. (And I have seen them, lazy and shiftless, hanging around the streets, mistook for niggers, and I have had my reverence mistook for blasphemy, too.) We had terrible fights.

The NAACP wants good jobs and kickbacks for the ignorant and the stupid. Affirmative action and female ejaculation some gratutitous and white approbation. I will not clench my face to meet the truth halfway.

We were two of a kind, horny third world graduate students, spitting images, funny and objectionable. (They allowed only consecrated virgins in the sacristy, brother, but I was a *child* and that is how I felt, fat old black lady on the maple syrup bottle; portrait of an artist as his or her own young man. I did not ask him if his old lady liked butter because I knew she did because the place where she turned from black to indigo she was perfect; she had sent a son to Howard University and it was a fatherless matriarchal society.)

From the land of Autocrat our mothers discuss us over the slow darksweet aroma of patient dreams.

Yes I had a black lover a Mr. X. I did not do his stubborn collar as he refused to do the mistress' shoes. (But you niggers got the vote before us bitches did, dear; and every Friday night we talked about the disenfranchised we had a brutal ugly kind of sex). The whole time I kept screaming is it true is it true he said close your eyes and think of—

Dublin, I said. yes Yes. It was.

You cannot deny the pornographic children, the enlarged genitalia, the rubber lips. You cannot deny your children play in the boarded rowhouses across the street, striking my car, overturning my bicycle, chasing the dog. You cannot deny the little bastard stole the dog and came to the door looking for his reward, without remorse or shame; his mother watching.

Shall I tell that big fat black lady on the Stoop, do not let your grandchildren play in hypodermic needles and the feathers are too dirty to touch? Tell her: your fucking little manchild gave each one of the grinning cats an enema with that junkie's swizzlestick and stole the dog? There is a murderer in the heart of each one of the disenfranchised and I knew her son had seen my VCR.

We discussed this whizzing in an alley or squatting for the Alyoop! We spared ourselves the ignominy of telling the other side. Some are impossible to love. I never wasted an evening telling him it was ok, ok. Our juices annealed.

My neighborhood is unsafe. I have chosen to live here. (Next door to an Arab who speaks despicably of vimen or is it venom or vermin.) Around these people my thoughts are not pure; I was led to believe that the poor had a sense of responsible suffering. Jogging by, so many of the nation's homeless have such dirty mouths and some of them come at you from their corners with their hands.

It is not all it was cracked up to be.

They lack tact and civility; my parents worked very hard, up from nothing: grew up in a well-meaning atmosphere with two babcocks, the hot and the cold. I could have buried my unwanted eggs on the ocean floor, dedicated my life to the unprofitable and implausible study of racists and the black dilemma, but have I come here, specifically, so I will not vote the Republican party or bake for the jaycees?

166

I shall have to stop apologizing for passing quarters only to the less obnoxious bag ladies and bag men. Should I have your accidental children we will climb into the phlegmatic pumpkin after midnight with its slanty squishy face and unfamiliar odor. (I will not stand by as the offensive child says to its mother, still a defiant teen, *who axsed you*?) We will take its picture in the bathtub, on roller skates, in a tutu, party hat, daddy's lap. Against the bulging backdrop of whorled white eyes I will ask them do you like bitters children? (chitterlins and greens, who has my hubcaps, who?)

Not mine, I told him. Too curly.

The butter principle.

Chutney, my next son, has a daddy and snarfs five fingers up into her mulching drooling (cavernous mouths).

We went to Chik 'n' Ribs, always had a mouthful of watermelons when we laughed and he agreed if necessary to come to my wedding as the father of my child. (Had I chosen to give her instead an avocado would she have been happier, visibly enlarged, would it have made life with her less bearable, more interesting, and if my grandfather had not gone to the GalapO(a,´)gos for good, had migrated back instead with the Candadian geese to the breeding grounds on a clear cool night in Rumford Maine with half a moon—his high-pitched bird sounds coming from the South—in the eternal V formation, would it have been different?)

After Chitterling and Ham Hock, I have Collard Green.

Human antipathy triggered a neurotic animal love and there was true solidarity at the liquor store; still a speakeasy or crap game at every corner and an old lady on every stoop or rocking in the upstairs.

Out by the reflecting pool, I kept feeding them gaudy pink popcorns to keep that duckdream alive.

You do not know enough to pet it love it leave it alone or kill it. Again it brushes up against you, some mangy creature with prophetic eyes, a past so hard and awful, you could never tell if it were safe to pet, or if its mother would never again touch it.

The gay men's chorus or an old woman's dream, the one blip or bubble that brings me up. To take the soft fallen crush of her blowsy black face, to bathe her in her own violet light—Hannah, Flo or Pearl—as she whispers indelicacies like *hushpuppy*, picking them like pieces of crepe off her bruised lip, because she ate for her children, the chitterlins and greens, spoke to me, and in putting silence aside, I was *Okra* for a day and where she turned from indigo to black she was again perfect.

You would have to love this little black Sambo child whether or not he was male or firstborn (those who believe in their own emancipation only) that is what I meant by the marbles, I told him. (we will have to name her *tar baby*, after our grandmothers)

He told me I was *all woman* and yes, I told him, he was *all man*. A funny thing to say but it was true (and when we argued the neighbors knew). And before I left the city I had sanity and peace of mind. I felt like Scheherazade, stupid fucking Scheherazade! And he was my white knight. As he felt Polyannish in a white tux and I felt cumbersome as his wife, we put this equivocating child on hold.

When the holiday is over the city streets are melted down. On good days you get your street poets and your troubadors.

Scolded for wandering off from his convalescence, home across the street, Pops is carrying on about his nurse. The bag lady talks to him, too. Friends. He tells her he is a fine magician. He puts the cats in the trash. ABRACADABRA. He lifts the lid and VOILA`. Cats. Yes, I, too, think he is a fine magician.

Pops sneaks out after lunch. He leaves the bag lady love letters in the trash. I don't think she reads too good but she smiles and knows what wrapper is his. He is not all there. Still, he is a fine magician and quite a gentleman to leave the bag lady love letters in the trash.

She is all excited to find it.

He drops his gums. Wets his trousers. Thar she blows.

Old geezer, a voice calls down from the upstairs. Abracadabra and Voilà, the bag lady squats to feed the gardenias. Tells Pops she is a conjurer, too. (Old fusspot she screams, fuddy-duddy. They don't need you.)

Pops has a mistress in the undauntable upstairs. Taking it slow down the fire escape to call out to the cats. Today is the holiday she says. They are coming to see me. Trudging through the slush and the bad weather.

Old woman catcha hypathermia out heah, Pops calls up, Whoop Whoop. Pops says that because she is always lost in the trundle of her big old coats. The kind the pickpockets wear.

Getcha beamend outa ma face mister.

But they are in love.

She calls out to the cats SOOEY SOOEY.

Pops has forgotten to finish his magic trick.

She cannot collect her cats today.

The kids are coming.

They won't come if the cats are there.

That's what they said.

They pay you to keep quiet. Your own children.

169

Come on down he yells up but she won't. I have seen how those young cabbies drive. Don't give an old woman time to get to the other side.

She keeps the corsage in her icebox. Freezer burn, brown around the edges (my eldest granddaughter's lawyer wedding). It no longer smells of flowers. She wears it anyway. It did, once.

From my deck I have seen other bag ladies too, rummaging for a place to wake up. Alley cats who turn the trash, pick through wrappers like gooey memories.

They never stay too long. They are bag ladies. So many things to do.

That's why we're all here, that's why we all came, we ran from Bar Harbor, the Fellinis of Maine, wearing our clothes like the badge of some exemplary pain. Underneath her garbage wraps there is a dignity there, unkempt and sad. Her loyalty made me sing. That is how, when she turned and hauled her gooey stash away, this gig got christened "The Bar Harbor Maine."

The sky begins where the flattop of tenement ends.

Maybe someday I will lift the lid and Voilá. Cats. And Abracadabra. More cats.

When you are watching from your tenement window, late, each afternoon, an old cat waiting to be fed, I come to you, mother, father; in the jingling troika of family and sleigh. Trudging through the slush and the bad weather. When you are an effort to remember when the snow is gray and backed up against the buildings when you wait for the bus with your giant shopping bags your pocketfuls of cats, toppling over on the sidewalk below, itty old bitties. Ants.

So many galoshes up in the air, a beetle on its back. Some kind of funny insect sex.

I will knock first and I will undress you, all the deadbolts that must be unfastened first; the up-to-the-neck blouse, the pantaloon trousers; I peer into you, while you peep back through the aperture, big as a pinhole, your chain still latched, knowing how dangerous I am, what a bother, your water boiling over and all the babies crying, the other phone ringing and all the business piling up. I have come to separate the socks. How to remove the static cling from cobwebs. Let me in. Mother let me in. Father it is me.

(The airs you give yourself not wanting to be bothered.)

It is a hospital mother full of nice people who help you void in pans and bless you when you sneeze. When you are too old for your upstairs tenement, your New England home, you come here, and I will hoist you up so you can say something and fall back on the bed.

Snow trickles down the inside windows like a postnasal drip.

The priest will press his face very close to yours. His breath smells like moths. His skin changes colors, all darks, browns and blacks, a kind of chameleon. He will tell you you are a big brave girl and crank down the bed. He licks the palate of his tongue and it is fuzzy, green. For one funny upside down moment you may need more time.

You are dying, Mrs. Dedalus, and this man is going to help you feel proud and happy, not ashamed or angry. Had you done it sixty-four years earlier the Rotary Club might have sent you to Disneyland first or sent the shortstop of the Yankees in to field you an autographed ground ball.

Rather, they have taken a collection at the parish, mother, to inform you compassionately that your breath stinks.

Portrait of a Girl

Before I leave mother I will minister my two forefingers to your cowlick and let you sit back for a nosebleed. I will store your urine in amber unmarked bottles I will put your teeth in when company comes and we will save your old coats.

I will wink at you father, and tell my children how far I have walked barefoot to school in the bad weather; we will keep the bourbon by the bed; you will not smell of moth balls, when your times come you grow old and picayune you begin to smell like babies and I will turn up the monitor so we can hear the bleep bleep and hear the tickertape fade off; I will lift you in and out of your wheelchairs, goad you over the hills fast faster then! yet! still! and you can pinch the maids who ripen the linens and blame the nurses for the taste of your food. I will tell you it is true, clear your random mind with golden bouillon, hang the alphabet over the bed, hold up flashcards, prompt the words and faces from under the bed and we will invent the language as we move along, buy you a metal detector and you can pick the beaches for abalone and a queer crunch.

The rare flush of your mother's cheek.

Pink albacore.

I will fetch the spaghetti pan, kiss your dementia on its rolling lips, saddle you into your bedpan. I will read to you from the good book Madeline let you babble, burble; turn your sores, hear your stories, hold you where it hurts, meet your mind halfway, where the tapwater drips, and I will stoke you up the opening in your johnnie coat and we will play patty cake and baker's man and you can repeat after me I will yes let you win, tuck you in, turn you over, and I will do your back, read you poems, close my eyes, behind your ears, your eyes, pull the plug, check your big toe tag twice, tickle your feet, back! back! I tuck you in, to whenceforth you came, born of your absurd notions to children who love you.

(There is a rufous-sided towhee at the feeder, again. And on and on.)

Father, shall I get that violin?

The hills are alive.

Because when I wanted to play up the nun's dress, in the lighthouse, fire, dumbwaiter, daddy's lap, when I said gimmee gimmee you said *no*; when I thought I might die in a barrel going down Niagara Falls, jowls of a grouchy jellystone bear, parachute won't open, belly of a whale, no way to hold on, trapped on an antarctican icefloat. When I was feminist, abolitionist, abortionist middle child, futile, polyglot in crib; you looked the other way. When I left home to live in the incubator with the baby chicks with the alligator in the murky bathwater, in underwater rock gardens, seat of a go-cart, sleeping standing up with the seahorses, mushing on the back of the family dog, the fog behind daddy's glasses, you said *go*. And when we said are we there yet *are we are we* you said *almost*. When I begged for a ride on the gondolas, Kong's palm, daddy's back, Moby's spout, Santa's knee, tilt-a-whirl, ponies, Huck's raft, horse and buggy, Cloud Nine, moonwalk; by pumpkin coach, rattling in with the milk bottles, back of the ice cream truck, hayride, dolphin fin, swinging vine, paper plane, peashooter, scooter, sp^3 hybridized state you said *we'll see*. When I begged to go: Transylvania, Berlin, Daddy's office, Jack's beanstalk, Bora Bora, the Vatican, attic, North Pole; Turkish Baths, Kremlin, Wild West, outside; Mars China Maine; to the beach, you said *take turns*. When I grew up to be: Gigantua, Gungadin, Sherlock, Abominable snowman, firstlady, pan, man; Easter Bunny, teeth fairy, your shadow, thy neighbor, Old Maid, chip off

173

the old block, Phylum Chordata, three wise men, a nun, what a woman, you said, *OK.*

Because it was to you whom I turned mother, father, when I was tortured and tired; persecuted, picked-on, ungainly, unsightly, cruel; middle child, spinning wheels at 7 or 27; when I was toppled over on my tricycle, reckless, morose; left for dead; tracked mud into the house, clodhoppers on table, talked back, tone of voice, elbows on table, wasted my father's money making up my mind, lost in the supermarket, got colicky, spit up, gave you gray hair, turned to you in love anguish, defiance; wore my face in my eyes, heart on sleeve, fumbled words, drunk, over my head, had a bubble, flunked calculus, failed life, bitten by dogs; bawling, begging, trashed the car, in the deep end, burned the brownies, cringed before company, begging for more. When I was stupid, slouching, has-been, nobody; sneaking spoiled, rejected by 40 medical schools; smartass; hiding lima beans in my napkin, let the dog go on the lawn, smoking cigarettes, going all the way; you sat on the roof of the house of the five senses, hard-working, honest, toiling like franciscan nuns.

I will get my birthing papers from the literary guild and keep them good 'ol state-a-maine plates; drive us all away in my chauffeur's cap the spinster daughter jingling in the family way smelling of rotting fruit we take all day, pick our meals from the discarded icebox chirping and shitting the monkey leads the way.

And like our grandmothers before us we live alone above the timberline for a long time painting with our toes, wetting and mulching, telling everybody they have a good 'ol Irish name (she couldn't see too well into the water where the ice was cracking Winthrop! she said she thought he was telling stories to the people gathered at the shore).

174

I drop a nickel in the violin case. Make the bag ladies
dance. Play me that song she says. Play me that song. She
has no teeth. Dance Pops Dance. She cracks a whip at his
feet with her horrendous smiles. But he won't dance. Too
proud.
A man can't help it if his arse leaks.

May I touch it, I asked?

Debbie Does Dublin: Hair of the Dog

"And all the little girls cried, 'Boohoo,
We want to have our appendix out, too!'"

Your Stradivarius, sir.
May I have a turn at the violin.
(I failed myself, irrevocably and immutably, for the last time.) Amen. So be it.
On with my life.
Put the quarter in.
Yes because I've never done a thing like this before as write a book in bed with a couple of eggs since Uncle's Lamplighter motel when I used to be pretending to be laid up with a sick voice doing his highness to make myself more interesting—to men. Droning over the chamberpot moo cows mooing shoo flies shooing looking at the gazette of holy objects panhandled goods button boots corsets love potions snake oil snow on the TV nothing left to give complaining that men is pigs why when he hit me it don't feel bad, exactly and when them abby and ann sisters goes and says *idiot* do what he likes why did you marry him I got to thinking well like the bishop said with the gals now riding the bicycle and the new woman bloomers the high school quivalency and the soaps and Monticello on the nickel the English Common Law is dead well I says to meself (the goose the gander the nature nurture for one for all): what an oafish unfeeling sensibility ee has don't ee

all them years they was writing ode to so and so come to find out straight from the horse's mouth Thesaurus they call it molly means Weakling, doormat, invertebrate, jelly-fish, milksop, Milquetoast, mollycoddle, namby-pamby, pantywaist, sop. (lay down and be dead nefarious monster I says to em all and that ain't the half of it)

Why do you bother to suffer so much you stupid woman thing and if I squeezed hard enough perhaps she would come to me at Lourdes too the femme fatale so I put away the menstruating paraphernalia and got on with it them wrack and boneshop questions, the thing with the violin (I heard an insect named Ludwig played the 3-legged piano with his numerous blind legs and those lady poets they was all trained at the Bellevue too.)

64 years later and I bust open like a pinata. I miss the scrotumsmelling biscuits Bloomie I don't need no new dress.

excuse the lady present

yes because they once took something down out of a woman that was up there for years covered with limesalts some woman said get thee to a warm bath so I did with a fat Roman Candle and done those Kegel exercises

O Jamesy!

I finally told him sitting up in his grave the carcass in me bed basted him turned him over next time you try to kiss me blarney stone looking like that there spectacle I'll av your blunderin arse catch me stream of consciousness kiss the gentle papacy but don't forget the profligate rest don't bother to excite me do you with your truss and big belly you'll av to knock off the stout at dinner fat ones are not so much the fashion 1986 Bloomie get yourself a melt-a-belt, polyurethane spacesuit, a vibrating arse machine kiss me do you with the blunt end of your tongue says ere got to get upside the giblet with it dumb hammerhead first man ooo kissed me under the Moorish wall my sweetheart eee was kidney too don't care a farthing do you you men if I can still ear the ineluctable munching of your breakfast in my ear Crunch Crunch ooo's there the *Weltanschaaung* who do you

bloody think suey! suey! out of my ear look at yourself in a
glass Aye! me little lolita limpet move the seaweed jailbait
let me see thine rolling eyes don't just lay there have some
allure think I should make a crèche ere in the covers for it
do you your cold feet smell like fritoes like the stale insides
of a vacuum cleaner isn't it simply sickening I should know
a man oughta be ashamed get your bloody boorish ands off
me mush! mush! out of me bed do some breathing exercises
change that mneumneu soft lights get me breakfast Bloomie
not to mention it you need a boudoir of your own, eyes
almondine, (so beastly bad in bed) take theeself to a warm
bath put the chain against the door wash yourself there
below with the glove I won't look at you you men with your
tackleboxes I know you're a fright bandit dog and a pirate
eye put on a clean shift and powder yourself smoke a pipe
like father's get the smell of a man do it simply to please me
bootlicking I want you pantcrawling in here 20 minutes
wearing only a rag sweater and the one blue eye

so another lady says to another *I hear she draws her
poison from the well* adjusting the overbite *A grandmother
dressed as a wolf* she retorts, a grandfather wearing his
wife's clothes have you checked your luncheon meats for
changing colors the crowd loves a hairy lady they all agree
barb wire snare I am my mother's daughter if that's what
you're all dying to know I whispered to the chameleon of
those I most wished to kill to the nun I keep in the closet for
a rainy day kiss her pearls and bunions mother of the novel
scallion breath for penance she will perhaps issue from her
autoerotic archives some postulate like celibacy or the
quantum theory painful intercourse her friend's initials I
am not a contortionist Sister I cannot say these things
c'mon baby she says let's play yes means no (she has eaten
perhaps cheese rarebit for lunch) OK then so I tell her them
Old Saxon words of pickled men who live inside the delicacy

of the frog fat man in my bed she has all day to detonate the
cancer paratroopers caught in the act of tandem the hand-
some head of ski patrol (I hear Sister creak against the
saddle as his boots come down brawny and big, from the
North) little ruggers in polo shirts their tiny valences on the
chest pocket holy clydesdales! what I dreamed with the
horse before God and my Country the whole Spanish
armada stomping through the endangered wetlands around
the maypole ruffled lamps do the fandango and in the
moors I ask them to dance the brothers grimm oh I have
been traipsed through the attic of Anne Frank also the
diaries of cruel children the boy I have just made bellcaptain
talk in the coffeeshop Ebeneezer there with the nose a self-
fulfilling prophecy too (she leans forward to breathe heavy
shearing forces the vague etiology of lower back pain she
wants to hear.

O Jamesy! By Jiminy! Hurry it up! I'll have my
Laryngectomy too Reaching for the Auld Lang Syne Bul-
garian or something it seemed like centuries we kissed the
way 2 whores kiss, making love for a man and ere I am
ready or not shaking out to them mops take your sweet
motherfucking time (cross the street) Bloomie to wait on me
hand and foot he's not ready Sister those men yes well then
plenty of other children's voices wafting out the oeils de
boeuf waiting to confess ouch watch where you plunk it
down to eat it horsy doo doo dream on give me another
lollipop I'll shut up OK mister I says to him into the car ever
seen anything like it Her majesty the king 12 inches Erect
Sister where did you get all your vainglorious little men
what makes you believe it as you do

Don't fool yourself I remain the irreverent nigger mother
I stoop to touch it Yo County 1986 cooking and sucking
please pick the cotton the stray diseased birdfellows a small
swaddling pimp the unrequited hair of the violin and

leading by the soft doe pad of my foot, send my family first
in graceful pulsing motions across the street taking my
bagchild from the bulrushes to this ere promised land I
must drink myself to death first no husband of my own
literary man about the house to fluff it up a cottontail you
must pat it one side then the other you must walk it walk
it away and away across the street one side then the other
you must send the children first tap dancers panthers
chicken shoeshine cat-o-nine watermelon blues and hook-
ers when they axkst I tell them white ladies from Dixie from
where I lain it was simply Humongus a fireplace in every
room what you think what I am some foot and mouth model
from the bottles of Vermont is it true? The baby has my
breath, don't you think. Bison breath, is it. Bless me little
barbarians. The answer is, doctor: like the boy of Equus
waiting for the horse to kick him in. A maltreated animal
of course I am his sister a veritable unknown I have just
finished my third triathalon as the darkhouse of Dublin too
nobody stops the streets to slap me five nobody calls me
brother in the jingle jangle male elite soul world yes well
only the confederate dream come on out with it Bloomie I
don't have zilch on what is it some psychosomatic sound
won't play on its own dip it in the rosin ere corner pocket
right in a little shoptalk
    We both loved it too very very much to have it a toucan
in its brilliant and abdicating colors we will teach it to
enunciate and we will beat it if it clumps one drop of blood
to the aggregate Others how can you dress a baby in
cellophane pants? Its tiny fingers climb the paper chroma-
tography column and stop, an asynchrony of colors (butter
cannot be all colors to all things)
    silly men little wallflower so weak and puling all men
get a bit like that at his age the Curse yes come to bed
brother I ain't going to murder you any moment you tired

Bloomie for the fat lot I care don't hide it with a cabbageleaf
(the man is beauty of course that's admitted) like hefner
and the catholic priests airbrushed madonna dugs devout
man statue alma mater of a nation imitation patties moist
meal in a pouch one of them catmouse problems is it it came
to me some epiphany afraid of the muscle of a mature
woman 1 man is not enuff for me yes because I couldn't
possibly do without it that long I am sure now 2 is not enuff
open up your Latin shirt with chest hairs I want them
imported from the black panthers or the far east haven't
you a pair of decent leather drawers an itty bitty slingshot
stuff it a bit no stand there Stately, plump. Take off your
shorts slow come to mother I need a real man one of them
vampire men to nick into it the pale heat rising off the nape
of my neck a quaff of garlic a bit of the blood drawn back but
slowly come to the crucifix backing away look scared my
Pamplona bull say it and bam and wham and not a word for
84 days what a man looks like with his two bags full show
me we're all so different like it or lump it painful slow
begging give me a tiny bit standing up in the sun naked like
a god or something beefcake slower than that I want them
pterodactyls swooning overhead take off your high-rise
Carters jellyrose make my heart go Clump Clump I am
chewing my shoelaces yes slide the hoof back and forth
against the floor like that ready to hump and bull faster!
yet! still! oh! (if you cannot write a book write a novella) a
bloody poem

But the line to the flume awful long Sister mostly
parochial brats fled from their charterbuses to see you must
I go on poor man suicide by the Vatican gas

it is all true he is the ghost of his grandfather I know, I
am his mafia princess she sleeps with the little boy the live
head of a horse a deposed grandfather and me, too. I have

learned to use my various little legs as airborne propelling flexor devices. Muscles, if you will.

I come across the finish line camelback with the center-piece already affixed to my head. Helen Gurly Brown. Icon. Cosmos girl. Daring to take away every little bit she gives. Before the Cosmos girl wakes up each morning she sneaks off into the bathroom to brush her teeth. The Cosmos girl feeds his feet three courses of snapdragons before she perks off to the office, the gabor sisters, nothing underneath, waving her well-orchestrated automations goodbye as if in automation off a homecoming float the Cosmos girl blinks on and off with the remote control she is welder by day turning cover girl tricks by evening a true lady gives her husband the fulbright and takes the doorprize getting home before the coach starts to smell to have her occasional orgasms waxing her legs and din din for exotic intellectuals and the man from Spam who keeps pulling the skin plasmolemma from his head while she screams and spit polishes the floor

Every man hides the face he wants to marry: in the floorboards moors or Lourdes.

for the fat hoot I give
hair of the dog
I give him his options love it or leave it
Crushed shells and the rose of abalone my holy break-fast too. Maestros, geishas, fishes and birds; not one egg.

Shall I go on, Sister, and pack the chowderhouses with the gray and speckle haired? This is 1986, the priests are molesting the altar boys you might sell the movie rights for Ulysses to Vatican III another small boy coming of age you were there first horsefly on the wall blind and too big with your alternate lifestyle

Father O'Leary his tubesteak hanging left

that tremulous big red brute of a thing where the
dickens is it my hole is itching always give me a good eyeful
back into the bathroom to brush them teeth doing that
frigging drawing out thing we're all mad to get on it
sticking up at me like a hatrack please just this once get on
with it I won't bother you again a nasty business for a man
I know what is it you want a French letter a few pence under
the pillow 8 poppies 5 killer tomatoes ha! ha! 20 pockets
aren't enuff for all my lies you men waiting for the Japanese
to take pictures to come at it with a lollipop so pigheaded
that's the kind of villainy they're always dreaming about
with not another thing in their empty heads they ought to
get slow poison the half of them from the well what is it
you're waiting for a fat suction lipendectomy Christmas
make it a natural size so as a woman could sit on it properly
all melted down into you like a suppository c'mon let's get
this lumpy old eyesore bed jingling like the dickens no more
blather about waking the infant tuckoo the fat lot I give up
with it encourage me open that shirt more hairs rabid at the
front yes you no woman would look at you twice make the
mickey stand for me all we want out of you the one thing
can't you sew some lace on your black scanties to show off
more of the human race more for me a whiff of the milkweed
glazed grass those golden boys at Margate Strand had
wings why aren't all men like that as a young boy you could
have got a pound or so a week as a wet nurse what between
clothes and cooking and children you can't do your holy
business now well it's all very fine for them and as for being
a man as soon as they're old they might as well throw them
out in the bottom of the ashpit I'll come home with the smell
of those painted goats once or twice ee won't stand for his
sort some filthy little shopboy it's a profession world's
oldest ye olde swapshop c'est la vie as my French goes,
cuckhold, I've got in with a forlorn spectacle, Sister, you

184

couldn't call him a husband it's 1986 god'll forgive me just this once or twice Sister don't you think? yes this bed is ambushed by chippendales a woman can't hardly help herself why I might attend the Russian ballet with the man in the window write to the personals MWF seeks afternoon delight pu pu for two who knows the Mrs. O'Leary with the funny Eye might invite me to some lesbo bebop brunch I could wipe my feet on daddy's mallard welcome mat home there's the pernambuco wood from Africa reluctant moslems masked men foot soldiers and insects too all a woman is to do lie down on a beach let the blue collar workers have a go at it the little ripsnorters of the moors gnomes with blunt bald heads limeys leprachans ghostbusters androids bushwackers too looking in (time herself is double-jointed) all of the uncomfortable positions Oh! pipefitters civil servants clouds puffing language looking up a bunch of trailblazing mini hahas Sister turn back the bed he Chief of the Laughing Moonwalk jello turned to sex surf 'n' turf chick 'n' ribs what is this vanillin substance hazing of the Sigman Nu can't help that Sister can we a bosom friend.

puff puff couldn't get away abominable Michelin man asbestos snow mitts orderlies and gourds

but I keep forgetting this birds pest of a thing pfooh men I want you pouty like a stripper silky like a schoolgirl would you put on them white waitress squeegies and walk across the room in them difficult to find half sizes yes put a magnificent switch of false hair on you wretch do yourself up keep tossing it all back like that Kitty O'Shea over a bit now under a blouse open at the front to encourage me (I'll help them college kids renovate the van when Dr. Gravity closes shop for the winter to walk them kites along the allotted bumps I'll catch a ride meet him for Christmas) no wonder we treat you the way we do you are a dreadful lot of bitches poor devils one of those mens diseases (some nemesis there in your parts) we might at least get a squeeze or two at a man going out to be drowned damn that stinking thing anyway c'mon I'll take anything for an excuse put your head anear my drawers that's what gives the men the moustaches I'm so savage for it god knows there's always something wrong with you 5 days every 3 or 4 weeks isn't enough usual monthly auction isn't it simply sickening Uncle he puts his long thing into my aunt Mary's hairy etcetera forever too keep your eyeglasses on eat guava peel a potato pretend you're one the them chippendales insects all over some elaborate phantasm on the beach dog edging to get up under your tacklebox do it the way Mrs. Mastrianna told me her husband made her like the dogs do it to beautiful white ladies mint juleps do it to a Nora Barnacle them ladies at the Bellevue too do it during Scylla and Charybdis middle of the afternoon that stuckup university student do it for him do it on 7 Eccles Street back of the caboose the Mrs. O'Flannery she'll strap one on for you the plastic doodads from the five and dime which one straps on (there's real beauty and poetry for you) say it say something dirty: *sacristy* I feel a bit of the wrangler coming on not to worry I'm a gentle woman and a christian owing to your condition eat it darling the French do.

The abbey is full of such good places for making love.

Up there in the stars I can see the Goodyear Blimp the whole floating novitiate with my azimuth compass the Rose Parade.

So the nun in the booth, from her kangaroo pouch, she fondles the tiny incriminations her tiny beads her *Handbook to Masochistic and Vicarious Living* through Christ with him in him sobbing and coming, a nun on a beach, all the demons rising out, Our Lady of—

omnibus cumulous she says *stop*

Hush.

186

Shhhh.

Again.

Why Sister it's me magma yes this here is molly bloom poet laureate ISO God it's OK you can tell me writer-in-residence Trinity College you know me molly back of the book it's 1986 you can do it kneeling standing on the Strand or in the Moors the his and hers monogrammed towels of Perpetual Motion the gargoyle, doctor, leaning over the crib was only me jingling the eyesore overhead yes me molly: sister brother mother father; the booze on the breath, the company coming well then yes mine too slouchy slutty ignorant has been nobody my grandfather a storyteller, too, like him I sign my maiden name a saint or the name of a whiskey emasculated the poor man his organ of Corti was much diminished should have let him lop off to get his Erection affairs in order left to her own offensive arguments she could not yes well then somebody dipped my grandmother in the India ink (Proteus, ll a.m.) she danced in the Irish spring upstairs nacheinander, then nabeneinander, walking around with that laughing look somebody bamboozled the old lady's savings it's not all true I sign my letters XXX I'm a bit of the old gray mulatta nag too it was the funeral of Paddy Digham followed by finnegan's wake I loved them both very very too much to remember I took an eyebrow and pencilled in the moustache what the Irish made the potato plastic for suck stone Paddy Digham the voice in your pocket comes forth itching always I'm not the mrs. nobody molly molloy.

Bend over Bloomie I think I've found the sienna crayon (burnt brown they called it, poop color) nobody wanted it five children in all.

like it or love it Sister I dump your celestial body like a lump on a beach forget the Strings g Spot remover pull a fishnet down over your face issue them small craft advisories and defile you all over again (oh yes the highways are full of hitchhiking prima donna who give good head) eat the funky cheese grow yourself a hair weave pardon me Sister it scares me to say it you must wash your mouth trenches first with Doves to speak of it the dead but once in awhile the mind chirps up some misplaced word fallen men tells you what you are really thinking puts the head of the donkey on the arse of a man and there you have it the dirty alphabet

You grow lean and wise like a panther years later running your crinkly fingers along the soft crèche of the binding rifling through the stacks what a job it is to get some hunchback monkey lackey dusted off these days to boost you upright through the stacks some vomiting epic elucidation was it Grendel or Grendel's mother alliterating in the grippe upstairs ten foot dragon tongues of flames some pagan infestation Family of Man a bloody shame (this man knows his Irish) nothing under M for molly M for me I must be the pseudonym the ghost relics of some old dying man's last breath the ichthyotic scalp of the fishwife crumbling driedflower between the yellowed leaves of his name a woman's age I marked the page and learned them words

(I am not Calypso a sea nymph who keeps Odysseus seven years on the island of Ogygia but the tiny cam wheels are turning

(who called my corned beef and cabbage the national dish a stinking pot au feu) what was it iambs or dactyls dancing in the Olde Upstairs how many little feet the pitter patter rhyme

Who is Hrothgar?

I don't know.

Who Hrothgar is.

I kept Excalibur by the bed. I eat them Danes and Swedes Geats too (cocktail franks) and singing Edelweiss

I would be back as hunchback scribe to avenge this headachy half-life Chief Big Foot Means You Know What I learned them gibberish words what with beer commercials the conflagration of souls it's what you men talk about chewing with your mouths open behind our backs along the Strand the crunch of wantons my own nana underfoot, yes I saw them gentle teeth along the shores and apertures of abalone— metemphychosis! I says to meself, bless the everloving abalone! It's someone's *grandmother*! and there they were the two of you making debonair conversation for yourselves you and Stevie I know about them periwinkles, starburst, over the rim is that what you want another man's bum or what have you a surrogate father kissing cousins consubstantial manhoods come poking home again late at night with the deer slit spreadeagled hung by the horns dangling from the dashboard of the Ford recreational vehicle how adept was she the Mrs. Stephen Dedalus at mounting you with her imitations the booze on his breath washing yourselves out to sea in a hot riptide of piss your wishful lady waiting to be quaffed chug a lug along down vive la difference some father son obfuscation wouldn't it be nice if you loved me really

or if you could possibly dream it when he made me spend the 2nd time tickling me behind with his finger I was coming Sister for about 5 minutes with my various legs round him I had to hug him after O Lord I suppose that is what a man is supposed to be there for or he wouldn't have made you the way he did so attractive to women all the pleasure we women get out of those men 1986 I can feel his mouth O Lord I must stretch myself O Jesus yes that thing comes on me yes now wouldn't that afflict you of course all the poking and rooting he had up in me then now what am I to do all fire inside fit to be tied.

molly she chose life in the great good indisputable Bloomsbook as readily as the deer chose his appointment in the tack room as readily as Marilyn Monroe chose life as a marine as I chose life in this disputed room yes you men part of the porkchop the wrack and boneshop you have loins, poetic needs, a classic sense of foaming manly glory beerdrinking gusto the neon flicking crest over the bar "Black" "Angus" "Steer" your mug a gavel at the bar feeds the whole town with one loaf its barley and hops we women groupies of all the men at the bar some fancy French dessert boring and stupid fillerup I says I want me stout Househusbande foaming manpower over the sides less of a lady and more of a life (why she's ere ain't she the queen of bawd herself badder than McHale's navy McHeath's rogues some platinum blond frothing out of the spit at Newgate rattling in with the milk bottles the men are yelling out Dugs! because I am a woman they says before I can say it they must send it first to Ireland before it can be imported back into the country hoof in mouth was it she's got they say Aye! Still throws like a girl Aye! At Yellowstone the bears only attack the menstruating women Aye! and sharks hate them too Aye! When women was women and men was men here's to it Aye! Aye! Aye!

Go manhandle the awful Truth sit on a potty chair singing climb into the blind beamend of a horse!

I yell back I'll av your henchmen too by the 1/4 lb. and medium rare. When I get me mad money go to the Berlitz night school I, authoress speak them dirty languages what would you like on your corndog usurper a little mustard mayo a little polyethylene my green pea

Aye! the stitches showing in your flattop Mr. corrosive pizza face Mr. family of man where your head ends the sky begins a flower Blooms in slow motion before your eyes molly sitting up

O Lady of the Gouged Eyes before the 6 Detonated horses before 3 white musketeers Bam Bam and Kong one curly hair and before God lay down your weapons open your blouse lay beside me and be bloody well done with it.

Better not make an all night begging the affair give it a bit of room poor devil for his cold feet room even to let a fart God poor creatures no analogous and miniature organ of his own flesh to go its own way spanking and whacking the blind thrust of the soul the Organ of this Chapter point your tongue Bloomie there Oh God! yes there now Kitch uh Bloomie no I'm what am I at all I'll be 33+ in September yes you can jump out of my cake a pair of lips you can open your hands flapping white into a dove Againe! Strong proud powerful feminine Bellows and Groanes don't you like me like that athlete coming over the triple jump insect I was Againe you can see the muscles working striations of them have I met my mountainflower man yes the man who counts the rabbits as they ricochet off his magical hands as he yanks them out one by one paws thumping yes now there's the man God! O may I lavish you with kisses buy you a new tie a little something under the pillow for yourself there there now I have proved by the love of the grand-mother the love of the man that's all there is you know sex death and the love of the grandmother he had never been so anonymous and how he kissed me under the Moorish wall and I thought well as well him as another oh! the blind thrust of the soul Againe! the awful pickled Irish flesh of the brogue slew Persues with the Gorgon eye like snow-flakes Bloomie the real ladies have em no two alike like potato chips we can't have just one I go through 5 sailors: 2, 3, 4 at a time why after Dedalus I take to his father and do his mother. If you can't bear it boys why close your eyes and think of Dublin pug dog all the voices drubbing in a fugue not unlike my grandparents all the voices speak at once 3/4 time AD-BC the ichy boot it sabotoges time in ways too difficult to imagine that Russian youth inventing punishment before the crime had no pot to piss in the fat lot of us I am it *Memoirs of a Dutiful Daughter* until now reluctant mother bonkers in France falling into the pastries vat du chocolat some invalid thinking she could take nothing but warm buttermilk and gums to the grave strong silent type raining cats and dogs without Sartre after I feel up his—I feel down his Other.

and this is finally how it feels from the inside out how molly her fingers smelled really when she told that yes yes lie and did she really spend all day on the chamberpot menstruating a head in its hands wishing she were you saying *you men* punctuated with all those queer upside down exclamation points calling the other bitches names

listen! it Buildes Againe ooo Jamesy! the crunch of the Weltauschanung underfoot mine! molly cheetah running not Irish enough is it for you gutteral female trouble shiver me timbers Againe a misplaced vine inverted monkey nerve funnylittle feelings all inside *me jane.* (I've been eating cotton candy in the upstairs) the feminary catching on yes means no one more time oh yes well then finish it off again yes make me spend one more time let me smear off onto your behind oh yes into your handkerchief I come down out of the alps Sister larger than life on a luge you can be pretending not to be excited you can keep my spunk on the handkerchief under the pillow you can shout out all sorts of things fuck or shit or anything at all only not to look ugly there ought to be some consolation for a man you can always wipe it off you just like a business my ommission and the sun shines for you today I tell him yes that's why I liked him because I saw he understood or felt what a woman was yes and my heart was going like mad and yes he said yes I will Yes I wanted to milk him into the tea well yes he's beyond everything I declare somebody ought to put him in the budget but I'm no marrying kind I'll marry money a swaggering jockey and hump the horse I'll spend like five sailors as I back myself sick and incontinent into the sea (if only I could remember one half of the things and write a book in the Modern English.

She would grow into her body like me at 64 jailbait in the third person Humbert Humbert's stream of consciousness and contempt a voice calling out its own name she finally shooting her own load into the chamberpot wringing her dishpan fishstink hands sliding off the chamberpot, to have and to hold to love and to serve like a growing family the freaks we become; to forge in the smithy of her soul the uncreated conscience of her sex tightening her bottom to let out a few smut words: molly smellrump or lick my shit

Portrait of a Girl

"And she turned out the light—
  and closed the door—
    and that's all there is—
  there isn't any more.
(But the biggest surprise by far—
on her stomach
was a scar!"

Postscript

What was wrong with Madeline.

1991 Madeline means Tower of Strength from the Hebrew too why she's a jew the ceiling crack had a habit of lookinglike an Easter rabbit whose habit was it knew so well how to frighten Miss Clavel

ich that was no appendix

"*Close Your Eyes and Think of Dublin: Portrait of a Girl*
may, therefore, be admitted to the United States."

Judge Wopner